AGAINST IMPASSABLE BARRIERS

THE TRAVELS OF SCOUT SHANNON

KATE MACLEOD

1

SCOUT SHANNON HUGGED her dog Shadow tight as she slowly drifted back down to the floor of the spaceship cabin. Shadow was napping, but Scout stared fixedly out the narrow band of viewscreens Liam had configured, which provided a 360-degree view of everything around the ship for her and her companions.

She felt like they were all trapped together in a glass droplet, unable to escape, only able to gaze out at the alien world that stood just out of reach, frozen in time.

Their spaceship sat in the center of a vast lunar plain like an immense reddish-black mirror sparsely dusted over with a layer of what looked like ash. Scout could see it clearly through the screen in the floor of the spaceship as she settled down onto it. It was almost close enough to touch, that ash. It looked like a fine grit, like one puff of air would send it scattering away in a rapidly dispersing cloud.

Alas, she could not touch it. And no puff of air would ever disturb it. But that was far from the most maddening thing about life on the moon.

Scout pushed away from the floor, floating back up to the cabin ceiling. She put a hand over her head to gently stop her momentum, clinging to the ceiling with her fingertips for the barest of moments before letting go to slowly sink back down to the floor.

It passed the time. But it was only a hair more interesting than lying in her hammock. And the time passed so very slowly.

The red-black mirror of the lava bed the ship rested on stretched for kilometers, nearly to the horizon on all sides. But the moon was so small that the horizon was much closer than the one Scout was used to back home. She could just make out the jagged outlines of toothlike mountains in the distance, but only when the planet shone brightly behind them. Otherwise, they faded into the black of the sky beyond.

No, it wasn't as immense as her home back on Amatheon with its endless fields of red-gold grain, but still, she longed to walk across it. She didn't care what was on the other side; she just wanted to start walking and keep walking and never ever stop.

As much as she longed for that, she knew her dogs needed it even more.

"Oh, Gert," Scout's friend Emilie said, her voice muffled by a hand over her mouth. "Not again."

"I've got her," Scout said, releasing Shadow to drift on his own and propelling herself across the cabin to where Emilie was buckled into the pilot's seat, running yet another pilot training program. Gert, who was quite smitten with Emilie, had been napping in the space around her feet, but apparently she had woken up to answer nature's call. Liam had helped Scout fabricate diapers for both dogs, but they were ill fitting, and the smallest gap let the contents escape into the air of the cabin. Gaps that happened every time the dogs scratched. And Gert scratched a lot.

In this case, it was urine, but that was almost worse than the other option. It quickly became a fine mist that coated everything.

"Just move out of the way and let the systems handle it," Liam said without looking up from his tablet. The words came out in an earnest, helpful tone, as if he hadn't been saying them over and over since they had landed.

"Sorry," Scout said, helping Emilie unbuckle from the seat and move to the back of the cabin.

"Can't be helped," Emilie said, but she still sounded annoyed. The systems had already detected the contaminant, and the filtration system was whirring to life, sucking the yellow droplets out of the air.

The systems could indeed handle the physical matter handily enough, but the smell? That always lingered. And accumulated.

Scout pulled Gert into her arms and carried her to the back of the cabin to change the diaper, Gert licking her face as if in desperate apology, although no one ever got mad. It was the one thing that made this whole experience of waiting to be rescued tolerable: everyone she was sharing it with was kind and nearly infinitely patient.

The lingering scent of dog urine was just as strong in the back of the cabin, but here it was, joined with a muskier smell. Geeta's perspiration. While Scout had her dogs and Emilie had her training program to keep her occupied, Liam had a harder time finding anything in his spaceship to help Geeta keep her mind off her sister. They were all always thinking of Seeta, stowed in a closet-like space in the floor, suspended in a medical stasis field that kept her at some undefined point between life and death. They were all worried. But Geeta couldn't focus her mind on anything but her grief, frustration, and guilt over not being able to save her sister in time.

In the end, Liam had found a way for her to focus on her body instead. He had attached tension bands to slots in the cabin floor and showed her how to use them to perform basic calisthenics, allowing her to keep her body strong despite the microgravity. She had taken to it with an almost obsessive zeal, working herself to collapse, then waking and starting the cycle over again. The others did a few exercises too at Liam's insistence, but it was Geeta who kept at it, pausing only to wipe the accumulation of sweat off her skin that couldn't drip away effectively enough in the microgravity.

She was at it even now, pulling again and again at the band, the muscles in her arms and back rippling under the sheen of sweat, her face set in a look of grim determination. As if she thought if she rowed hard enough, she could somehow get the ship they were waiting for to arrive just a bit faster.

Scout sealed the diaper as tightly as she could, then let Gert go. Gert launched herself at Shadow, tackling him briefly before he ricocheted away from her. The dogs were forming some sense of how to propel themselves around the space inside the cabin, but Gert hadn't yet worked out a way to get a proper wrestle in with Shadow.

"I'm making… tea," Emilie said. She always left that hesitation there before she said the word "tea." It was as close as any of them got to complaining. But then the tea Liam had in his stores was meant to last forever, which as far as Scout could tell meant that it always tasted like it had been stored too long, the leaves little more than dust. Still, it was better than nothing. "Anyone want any?" Emilie offered.

"Sure," Geeta said through gritted teeth, redoubling her efforts with the tension band.

Liam looked up from his tablet, but before he could answer, they all heard the soft warning trill from the midrange scanners.

"Display," Liam said, and the ship's computer dimmed the lights, projecting a hologram of the moon in the center of the cabin.

"There," Emilie said, seeing the dot of movement in the far corner of the space.

"Just passing by?" Scout guessed. She was speaking in a whisper, just as Emilie and even Liam had, although there was no way for anyone outside the ship to hear them.

Then another dot appeared next to the first, and then a third. They were flying in a triangular formation, but not towards the moon.

"Transponders?" Liam asked. So far, the few ships that had passed close enough to the moon for the ship to detect them had been flying without transponders. Smugglers who had sneaked past the barricade, Liam had assured them. Not friends, but not actively searching for them, either.

"Yes," the computer answered. "A security patrol from the colony ship *Tajaki 47*."

"Looking for us?" Liam wondered aloud.

The computer knew he wasn't really asking, since there was no way for it to know if that was true, and it remained silent.

"They aren't heading this way," Scout said.

"With all the smuggler ships we've watched go by in the past few days, I'm not sure what is more surprising: not seeing a patrol before now or suddenly seeing one today," Emilie said.

"It could be something else," Geeta said. She had stopped exercising when the hologram appeared and was studying it intently. "They aren't heading towards us, or in the same direction as the smuggler ships. It looks like they're heading for the barricade itself."

"Escort, maybe?" Liam said.

"Can the long-range sensors detect anything?" Scout asked.

"Only the barricade itself, which is unchanged," the ship's computer answered her. It still creeped Scout out when it did that.

Liam had introduced them all to his computer as if it were a person, and he encouraged them to interact with it as the first step to adjusting to life in Galactic Central with all its modern technology. Geeta and Emilie took it all in stride. Only Scout lay awake at night, somehow viscerally aware that the computer was listening to her breathe just in case she should ask it a question.

"Where is the flagship now?" Geeta asked. The hologram contracted, the moving dots winking out of view as the glittering array of the barricade came into view all around them. Liam had told them it was invisible to the naked eye out in the black of space, but the ship displayed it as an intricate web of light forming a sphere around Amatheon and its moon. Passing through that web would alert the ships that guarded the barricade, including the massive flagship that roamed the barricade's interior with no set pattern.

"There," Emilie said, once again the first one to find the subtle gleam of light that marked the ship's position against the brighter web. "I don't think they are heading towards it at all."

"No," Liam agreed. "But where are they heading?"

"Your friends?" Scout asked, scarcely daring to hope that their long wait might be nearly over.

"If they were close enough for the systems at *Amatheon Orbiter 1* to detect, they would have called by now," Liam said.

"Maybe they're in trouble," Scout said. "Maybe they need help."

"Should we go?" Emilie asked. Her voice was still pitched low, but the corners of her mouth were starting to curl up in that maniacal grin she had.

"Nothing is being detected," Geeta said. "No motion, no transponders. We would likely just be revealing our position for nothing."

"Geeta is right," Liam said. "We're safer where we are."

"Maybe you should message them again," Scout said.

"Messages are dangerous," Liam said. "Once you broadcast it, anyone can intercept it."

Scout nodded glumly. She knew he was right, but still felt like it was probably worth the risk. She would feel better knowing exactly where his friends were and how much longer they would have to wait.

"I'll send a short one," Liam said. "Once these ships are gone. When the coast is clear."

"This situation can't go on forever," Geeta said, wiping the sweat from her face with a thick towel. "The barricade isn't supposed to be up forever."

"But it's been there for years," Emilie said. "It *feels* like it will be there forever."

"It won't come down until the courts have settled the matter of who is the rightful owner of the planetary system," Liam said.

"But the courts are so far away," Geeta said. "How will we know when they are done?"

"You'll know because you'll be there," Liam promised her. "You'll be right in that court at Galactic Central when the tribunal makes its ruling."

"But how can we know they haven't decided already?" Geeta persisted.

"These matters drag on for decades," Liam said. "Both sides of the Tajaki trade dynasty have access to the best lawyers in the galaxy. With all their machinations, legal moves, and countermoves, this could go on for years to come."

"We're going to be waiting to testify for years?" Scout asked.

"No. As soon as you arrive, my friends can start filing motions of their own. That changes things."

"Are your friends in the same league as the Tajaki lawyers?" Geeta asked.

"No," Liam admitted. "But it won't matter. Both sides of the Tajaki dynasty have equal claim on the planet. That's why neither side can get the upper hand. But you all have a different claim. You're not claiming ownership; you're claiming sovereignty. One way or another, that will be faster to resolve."

"So nothing changes until we get there," Geeta said.

"But we're still stuck here, waiting," Emilie said.

"Not for much longer," Liam said. "We'll be on our way soon, I promise."

Then the hologram of the moon and its surroundings winked off without anyone giving the computer a command. Where the moon had once stood, there was now a woman standing in the middle of their ship's cabin, arms folded as she looked sternly down at Liam.

"I would advise against making such promises, Marshal. You won't be around to see them through."

2

THE WOMAN WAS TALL, at least half a head taller than Liam. Shiny black pants clung to thickly muscled thighs, and her long white shirt stretched over broad shoulders. Her salt-and-pepper hair was pulled back into a tight bun at the nape of her neck. The wrinkles in the skin around her eyes said she was prone to smiling, but the scowl she was currently directing at Liam was anything but amused. The tailoring of her shirt suggested a uniform, but if she wore any insignia, it was covered by her crossed arms.

At first, Scout wondered just how heavy this woman must be that she could stand upright in the microgravity. Liam, with all the body modifications that came with being a galactic marshal, could stand and even walk around the cabin with only the slightest of springs to his step. Scout and the others had given up trying to walk; it inevitably ended in ricocheting between floor and ceiling. The woman wasn't moving, but she looked like if she did, it would be with the unstoppable forward momentum of a tank.

Then Geeta reached out a hand to touch the woman's elbow, and her fingers passed through it. The woman didn't even react, but Emilie and Geeta were as stunned as Scout. The ship's moon hologram had been beautiful, detailed, and plain to see from every angle, but there had never been any question that it was just a projected image. This woman, though, looked real. As if she were physically there in the cabin with them.

Only she wasn't.

Scout looked over at the two dogs, who were watching with only mild interest. The very opposite of their usual reaction to the sudden appearance of strangers.

"Captain Salvo," Liam said.

"Save it," the woman said, holding up a hand against whatever words he had been about to say. "Where's Bauer?"

"Dead, sir," Liam said. The sternness melted from Salvo's face.

"You're certain?" she asked.

"Yes, sir."

"That is a shame. It wasn't this McFarlane fellow? He didn't seem capable of getting the drop on a marshal like Bauer."

"No, sir. It was an assassin, trained and with body modifications. Bauer wasn't even the target, just collateral damage. The political situation here—"

"Thanks to you and your partner, I'm far too aware of the political situation here," Salvo said, the sternness back in her tone and the furrow of her brow. "I had to come here personally to extract you in order to defuse some of the tension in this political situation. Personally, McGillicuddy. I didn't just have to leave the office—and you know how much I hate leaving the office—I had to leave Galactic Central."

"I *am* sorry," Liam said. "I owed Bauer far more than she asked of me. I had to come and see her final wishes through."

"McFarlane isn't with you?" she asked, her eyes sweeping over the cabin. Scout flinched as those steely blue eyes rested on her for the barest of seconds before moving on to Geeta and Emilie.

"No, he died as well," Liam said. "Bauer asked me to see to her protégé, Scout Shannon." He held out a hand, directing those eyes back to Scout.

She fought the urge to squirm as the woman looked her over, or to explain that she didn't look a thing like her usual self. All her clothes were borrowed and mostly not to her style. Even her hair was different, a necessary part of the disguise that helped her escape the space station with Geeta and Emilie despite an entire security force hunting for her. Gone were the long honey-gold curls so reminiscent of her mother's hair. In its place was a short orange mop of hair, no longer holding its shape without the elaborate system of hair products Seeta's friend had used to set it.

The microgravity didn't help either. But at least her hair was too short to get in her eyes.

"I have to remove you from this system," Salvo said, returning her attention to Liam. "Just you. No others. I'm here with a ménage of tribunal enforcers." She paused, and Scout sensed that those tribunal enforcers, whoever they were, must be very near at hand. Salvo had the air of someone carefully choosing her words while working hard not to shudder.

"Yes, of course," Liam said. "Are you coming here, or…?"

"We're in orbit over you even as we speak," Salvo said. "Don't worry about nothing appearing on your sensors. Apparently, that's normal for this type of tribunal enforcer craft."

"But what about us?" Scout blurted out.

"Something will have to be arranged," Salvo said with a frown. "We can't just leave you there on the airless moon."

"Can't you take us with Liam?" Geeta asked. Scout noticed she was standing straighter as if at attention, holding fast to the back of the pilot seat behind her to keep from floating away and ruining the effect of standing at attention. And that little edge was back in her voice, the one she used when forcing someone to acknowledge her authority as an ensign working in security on *Amatheon Orbiter 1* and not get hung up on her youth and diminutive size.

"It's not safe for them here," Liam said. "I can explain in more detail, but that's the gist of it."

"They can be moved, but only to another location within the barricade," Salvo said. Her eyes darted off to one side, and Scout guessed she was looking to one of those tribunal enforcers to confirm her words before looking back at Liam.

"There is no safe place for us inside the barricade," Geeta said. "At least two groups of people are hunting for us."

"It's all right," Liam said quickly. "Give me a minute to settle things here and I'll go with you."

"We're descending now," Salvo said. "A minute may be all you get."

The hologram winked out of existence as abruptly as it had appeared.

"How could she do that?" Emilie asked wonderingly. "Did she bypass the ship computer's security protocols?"

"As a captain, she can do a lot more than that," Liam said. "She could have fired our rockets remotely and just brought us to her if she wanted."

"Why didn't she?" Scout asked.

"She knows more about what's happening than she's going to let on with a ménage of tribunal enforcers all around her. She has to obey all orders to the letter, but every bit of wiggle room she can find she's going to use. Like coming here personally and giving me as much advance warning as she could."

"Warning to do what?" Scout asked. "Are you going to run away?"

"No, that's not possible," Liam said. "I was hoping my friends would get here first, and that I could turn myself in back at Galactic Central. I'm afraid me being arrested was always going to happen. It was just a matter of when."

"What happens to us?" Emilie asked.

"You'll go on as we have been, waiting in the ship," Liam said. "It's not much longer now, surely."

"You're leaving us alone?" Scout asked.

"Alone together," Liam said. He turned away to look out the front screen of the ship, but Scout saw nothing out there. He turned back to the three of them waiting anxiously for him to explain. "We haven't been wasting our time here, have we? You all know how to operate every system on this ship, and Emilie even knows how to fly it. Geeta knows how to monitor her sister in stasis and make adjustments if needed, and Scout has all the tools of a galactic marshal, save the gun. You're as prepared as I can make you."

"You knew this would happen?" Scout asked.

"I knew it was a possibility," Liam said, looking out the front screen again, this time his eyes lower down towards the lava bed, but again Scout saw nothing.

"What's a tribunal enforcer?" Geeta asked.

"They are officers of the court. They're a strange lot, all from the same planet near the galactic core. The planet was settled by humans centuries ago, but there was something in the soil or water or air that changed them over time. They are something other than human now. Some say they are telepathic. All I know is that they don't talk much, just watch you with these piercing eyes, and they are all damn unsettling. But you don't need to worry about them. I know 'enforcer' sounds scary, but unless you are attempting to violate a court order, 'observer' would be a more apt description of them. And there would be no reason for you to violate a court order."

He looked out the window again, then went to the back of the cabin and retrieved a bag from one of the cabinets. Personal things, Scout guessed.

"Crossing the barricade violates the court order," Geeta said.

"Which is why you're not going to try to do it without my friends' help," Liam said. "Just wait here for my friends, the Torreses. John Carlo and Mary Grace. You know what they look like, and you know the sign and countersign."

"Justice," Geeta said.

"Sovereignty," Emilie said.

Liam gave them a nod.

"Don't you need to turn in the belt?" Scout asked, touching the buckle of the double belt around her hips. The equipment on that belt had come in handy on more than one occasion, but technically, it was never hers.

"No, keep it," Liam said. "Gertrude left it to you."

"She never said that," Scout said. Her cheeks flushed; she had as much as admitted to reading all of Gertrude's personal correspondence to know such a thing for sure.

"She gave you access," Liam said, looking almost puzzled that Scout hadn't known that.

"How… when?" Scout asked, even more confused than he was.

"She must have gotten a sample of your DNA at some point?"

"Blood," Scout said. "She tested me for poison."

"She used that to give you access," Liam said, checking the contents of his bag briefly before throwing it over one shoulder. "If she hadn't, you would never have been able to remove that eyepiece, let alone use it."

"But that doesn't make sense," Scout said. "I handed the eyepiece to someone else to look at the tablet. Gertrude had never met her. How did she have access?"

"She could use the eyepiece because you handed it to her, and she could see only what you had summoned onto the tablet for her to see. She wouldn't have been able to use it in any other way."

Scout had so many more questions, but something clanged against the hull, echoing through the cabin.

"They're here," Emilie said. "Five bald people in long blue robes and your boss. How are they just standing... oh, I see. Clever. I guess it's safe to open the door now."

"Yes, it's time to go," Liam said.

"Wait!" Scout said, rushing to catch Liam's arm. He had to catch hold of her shoulder as well to keep her from tumbling over him. Once he had her steady, Scout pulled a battered tablet out of one of the belt's many pouches. "This was Farlane McFarlane's tablet. There might be evidence on it. Maybe a way to get some of the money he stole back to his victims."

"Good thinking," Liam said, tucking the tablet into a pocket on the side of his bag. "You three are going to be all right. There's not a doubt in my mind about that."

"I wish we were going with you," Geeta said. "If they knew about my sister..."

"It wouldn't change anything. I'm sorry," Liam said.

"I wish I were going just to get a closer look at that ship," Emilie said, still gazing out the window. Her voice was full of wonder and awe, the sort of thing that would usually bring a smile to Scout's face. Emilie's enthusiasms were sometimes hard to understand, but they were so genuine they were infectious.

But at the moment, it was all Scout could do to blink back the tears as Liam pressed the button to open the door and lower the ramp. At least this time he was walking away of his own free will, not dragged off to be tortured by parties unknown.

But the result was the same. Scout was on her own in a world she barely understood.

Then she felt a hand on her arm and looked up at Geeta bravely attempting to summon her first smile since her sister had been hurt. It was a wobbly smile, but it was enough. Scout knew she wasn't alone. Not this time.

Emilie had moved from the window to the top of the ramp to look down at the cluster of figures awaiting Liam. The five with bald heads and blue robes formed a circle around him and Salvo as he stepped up to her, hands extended as if ready to be shackled. She waved away his gesture with a grimace of annoyance, then led the way back to whatever ship had brought her there, the five tribunal enforcers maintaining a disciplined phalanx around them.

None of them had so much as glanced up at the three girls still in the ship.

"I can't wait until we get to Galactic Central," Emilie said as she pressed the button to redraw the ramp and close the door. "You should see their ship! It's like living crystal, gorgeous and fluid. They just extend part of it like a pseudopod to attach around the doorway of our ship. Better than an airlock. It's amazing!"

She went back to the window to watch the ship lift back up into the starry sky, but Scout couldn't summon much interest in the wonders of a world that felt further away than ever. Neither could Geeta, who was staring fixedly at the part of the floor that had just been a ramp, biting down hard on her lip.

Scout wasn't used to being around people, not since her family had died when she was ten. She really didn't know how to be a friend. She didn't know what to say, so she just put her arms around Geeta and hugged her tight. Geeta stiffened momentarily, but then she relaxed and hugged Scout back.

They would be okay, Scout decided, as the two of them slowly drifted across the cabin. As long as they were all together, they would always find a way to be okay.

3

THE DAYS PASSED, or rather, time did. They slept when tired, woke when rested, and ate when they were hungry. The sense of being on the same schedule with each other even faded away. Emilie seemed to be always awake, getting up from the pilot's chair only to answer nature's call or help herself to another meal from the still nearly full cabinet. Geeta worked out to the point of collapsing but only slept for an hour or two before untangling herself from her hammock and stumbling/floating back to the tension bands.

Scout tried to keep to a normal schedule, but it was impossible to know what that was when the world outside the windows never changed. There was no day or night, a fact that Emilie and Geeta were quite used to, having spent their entire lives on board an artificially lit space station. Scout was used to the sun, to always knowing how much time remained of the day by its position in the sky. She knew the patterns in the movements of the stars at night as well. But here it was all different. The sun seemed stuck just over the peaks of the mountains behind the ship, and the stars were in configurations she had never seen before.

The only measurable change was the planet slowing rising over the horizon in front of the ship. It seemed unmoving hour to hour, but over the course of the growing number of days, it was becoming ever more prominent, lighting up the interior of their craft like a full moon over the prairie.

"It's getting bigger, isn't it?" Scout asked on a rare occasion when they were all awake at the same time.

"Closer," Emilie said. This moon isn't tidally locked."

"What does that mean?" Scout asked.

Emilie shut down the pilot training program she had been running to give Scout her full attention. She started moving her hands in gestures that made no sense to Scout. "We're orbiting just like the planet is, only slower. The sun is setting behind us, the planet is rising in front of us. Not at the same rate, though. Do you want me to make a model?"

Scout winced. Emilie would happily explain it over and over until Scout understood, but that could take hours. Better to focus on the important part.

"So we're not really on the far side of the planet anymore, or at least we won't be soon," Scout said. "Are we still actually hiding?"

"I don't think anyone really bothers with the moon," Emilie said. "All the satellites and space stations have a much closer orbit."

"It was thoroughly surveyed by our ancestors when they first arrived," Geeta said, wiping slick sweat from her arms with a grungy towel. They had no effective way of doing laundry, which was becoming quite apparent, but no one was going to tell Geeta to stop exercising. "They found nothing worth mining, and with most space stations being under spin to simulate gravity, there was no reason to put an outpost here."

"But if someone was still looking for us?" Scout asked.

"Would they be?" Emilie asked. "They chased us away from the space station, but they never fired shots."

"They were shooting at us in the hangar before we took off," Scout said.

"Maybe us being gone means we're as good as dead to them," Emilie speculated. "We're not there anymore to make trouble. It might not be worth the resources it would take for them to keep hunting for us."

"So, are we safe, then?" Scout asked.

"We have to stay here," Geeta said. "This is where Liam's friends know to find us."

"I wasn't suggesting we leave the moon," Scout said. "But maybe we want to move the ship away from the rising planet, so we're back on the far side."

"I think we're better off where we are," Emilie said, adjusting her glasses. Since they had left the station with its network behind, she no longer had endless fonts of information available to her, and Scout wasn't even sure she needed the lenses to correct her vision. It was more like she wore them out of habit and kept tapping at them when she was thinking, also out of habit, although that often—like now—ended in her making a frustrated scowl.

Scout supposed that to Emilie, it was a lot like being blind.

"I agree," Geeta said. "I'm worried if we try moving the ship, we might draw attention. Liam put us down here with mountains all around us. I doubt we'd find a better place to hide."

"I guess you're right," Scout said.

She just wished their ride would get there already.

In the middle of what Scout considered her night, when she was tucked inside her hammock with both dogs packed in around her, the midrange sensor alarm sounded. She squirmed around until her head was poking out of the canvas.

Emilie had already activated the hologram and was floating away from the pilot's seat, searching for what had triggered the alarm. It was another trio of ships in formation at the edge of the display field. Scout and Emilie watched them as they cut across the border of the sphere and disappeared.

"Same direction as the last group?" Scout asked sleepily.

"Similar," Emilie said at a whisper, since Geeta was still softly snoring. "Not identical. Perhaps they are increasing patrols."

They stayed as they were for several long minutes, waiting for something more to happen, but nothing did. Emilie stretched and then sailed to the back of the cabin for another meal packet before heading back to her seat. Scout tucked her head back into the warm space and calmed the fussing Shadow with a hand on his head.

The alarm went off again some hours later. This time Scout untangled herself from the hammock and sailed out into the center of the cabin. Geeta had been exercising, but she released the bands to help look for dots of motion.

Two sets of three ships now, flying in separate formations. One was heading in the same general direction as the last two had been, but the other was on a path that was going to take it close to the moon, on the way down to a closer orbit of Amatheon.

Emilie was looking up through the windscreen, and Geeta and Scout drew close behind her, hovering near her shoulders. None of them said a word as their eyes searched the star field.

Emilie saw them first, raising a hand wordlessly to point out three all but invisible specks moving through the black. There was no sound, not from the ships and not from the three of them as they each held their breath, watching the patrol ships fly by.

For a moment they stood out in sharp detail, the blue-white glow of Amatheon behind them giving them a sharp silhouette. Then they disappeared, swallowed up by that light.

"Not looking for us, I guess," Emilie said.

"Were they close enough to see us?" Scout asked.

"Just sitting here, running nothing but life support, in the shadow of those mountains?" Emilie shrugged.

"They weren't looking for us," Geeta said. "I don't have any flight training, but that didn't look like a search formation. It was just a patrol."

"Okay, but what happens when the planet rises a little higher and that mountain range is no longer between us and the Star Farer space traffic monitoring satellites?" Scout asked.

Emilie touched her glasses and grimaced, then remembered the ship's computer was there to help with just those kinds of calculations. "Ship, how long until we're no longer in that mountain's shadow?"

"Four days," the computer answered, providing a hologram as if someone had asked it to show its work.

"Surely they'll pick us up by then," Scout said, but her voice didn't sound as hopeful as she had expected.

"We're getting to the point where we might have to consider that something went wrong," Geeta said.

"We're not there yet?" Scout asked.

"No," Geeta said, but if she had any confidence in that answer, it was drowned out by her ever-growing exhaustion.

"Four days," Emilie said. "We can wait here until then, but in the meantime, we need to come up with some other options."

"We can't try crossing the barricade," Scout said.

"No kidding," Emilie said with a humorless laugh. "You never looked out at that ship, but its hull was crystal clear. Like, invisible. And it never appeared on any of the ship's scanners. The sky could be full of those, and we'd never know until we were surrounded. No, the barricade is not a viable option."

"We can't go down to the surface," Scout said.

"Why not?" Emilie asked. "There are lots of places that are sparsely populated, some that are even unpopulated. We could hide forever down there."

"But the coronal mass ejections," Scout said. "They have been stronger than ever, and more frequent since you Space Farers started taking down the satellites that made the shield. I don't mean *you* guys," she hastily added. Geeta and her sister, along with Emilie, had been working against those actions even before they met Scout.

"We could find a spot near a… protective place? A cave or something," Emilie said, but Geeta just shook her head.

"We move the ship back," she said. "Back to the dark on the far side of the moon. Then we wait again. This is where the Torreses will be coming for us."

Emilie bit at the side of her thumb, clearly thinking something, although she'd said not a word.

"That does sound like the safest plan," Scout agreed, and Geeta floated to the back of the cabin to get a bulb of water.

Scout pulled herself closer to Emilie. "You're thinking something else," she said in a whisper.

"Maybe," Emilie said, words muffled by the thumb still against her mouth. "I'm worried we'll be seen. Geeta's plan is the safest if we can stay hiding, but if we can't? I want to have another plan."

"I don't think I'm going to be much help," Scout said.

"Don't worry about it," Emilie said, leaning forward to start another training program. "I think I have an idea. Or at least the start of one. Probably won't even need it. I'm sure they'll be here to get us before we'll even be in danger of being exposed."

"Yes, I'm sure they will," Scout agreed.

But four days later, the dust-covered lava bed behind the ship was gleaming brightly in the reflected light from the planet, the shadows of the mountains like jagged teeth stretched over the plain.

And just behind them, one sawtooth was marred by a smooth arc. The light was touching the very apex of the ship. It was time to move.

"Taking off, gliding back, and landing should be easy enough, right?" Geeta asked.

Before Emilie could even answer, the ship alerted them to movement, a strange repeated beeping that was not its usual quick tone. The hologram flickered to life, and they saw why. Six squadrons of ships were now passing close enough to the moon to set off the alarms. Four were heading towards the barricade, but two were on a path to pass right overhead.

"They'll see us," Scout said. "The light is hitting the top of the ship. The ship is like chrome; it shines like starlight. They can't miss us!"

"We can't move now; they'd definitely see that," Emilie said. "We just have to hope if they do see a gleam, they'll assume it's just part of the lava bed reflecting back at them."

"The lava *is* like glass," Geeta said. "Maybe they will."

They fell silent, gazing up through the windscreen until the faint specks of the ships came into view. They flew overhead, never changing formation or making any move to stop or land.

They all released their breath at the same moment when the outline of the ships had been swallowed up by the brightness of Amatheon.

"We have to leave," Scout said.

"They might not have seen us," Geeta said.

"They might have and reported us to their command," Scout said. "Just because they didn't come after us themselves doesn't mean no one will. They clearly already had a place to be."

"We can't move," Geeta said. "How will the Torreses know where to find us if we do?"

"I have a plan," Emilie said. "It's a bit tricky, but I think I can pull it off."

"Pull what off?" Geeta asked.

"Look," Emilie said, zooming out the hologram using the controls on the console. Then she tapped something else and tiny dots glowed a bright green, scattered throughout the cabin in a chaotic band.

"What are they?" Scout asked.

"Those are abandoned space stations," Emilie said. "When the population fell after the war, these were left unmanned. Most don't have spin, but this one here does," she said, making one green dot flash.

"It looks close by," Scout said.

"It *is* close by," Emilie said. "Close enough where we can watch for activity around the moon. The moment anyone arrives who could be looking for us, we'll know and can send a message. We can be sure it's really the Torreses before we expose ourselves."

"But won't we be risking somebody seeing us moving? Somebody connected to one of the groups hunting us, or just someone who just reports seeing us, and that report gets back to our pursuers?" Geeta asked. "Hopping over the surface of the moon is one thing, but that is crossing actual space. Space we've seen these patrols crossing repeatedly. Watched space, I think we'd have to assume."

"I can do it," Emilie said with firm confidence. "The ship's computer and I have been working all the angles for days. I can fire our rockets here to get away from the moon, but just one burst. Then I kill the engines and momentum takes us straight there."

"That will work?" Scout asked dubiously.

"Yes," Emilie said. "It's just physics."

"But someone might see us," Geeta persisted.

"Only if they're looking, and if they know exactly where to look. Our rocket will flare, but only close to the lunar surface. The same as if we changed position to move further back along the far side. So that risk is the same. Crossing open space, with our engines off, we'll be pretty close to invisible."

"Pretty close," Geeta repeated.

"More than close enough," Emilie said. "We might show a little bit of heat, we might reflect a bit of light, but it's nothing anyone would notice unless they were actively scanning every kilometer between here and that station looking for us."

"And if they were actively looking for us here, we would have seen a lot more ships," Scout added.

"Exactly," Emilie said.

They both looked to Geeta, who was biting her lip. Scout was all too aware that in the cabinet under the toes she was standing on was Geeta's sister Seeta, deep in a stasis from which she might never come out.

"All right," Geeta agreed at last. "Show me how it's done."

4

THEY ALL SEEMED to be thinking the same thing: there was no time to waste. Scout gave the dogs water from a bulb, a process they were getting used to if they didn't exactly like, then tucked them together into the same cabinet they had been in when they had landed. The netting of tape was still there to hold them inside; she just had to add a few fresh strips to keep it closed once more.

Geeta buckled into the seat beside Emilie and at Emilie's instruction brought up screens that showed her what the ship was detecting around them. Nothing so far, but she wanted to be prepared.

Scout made a final pass around the cabin, retrieving an empty water bulb and a lone towel and securing them in a cabinet, then came to float between the two seats. She had one of Geeta's tension bands connecting her belt to a loop on the floor, but mainly kept herself in place with a hand on the back of each of the two seats.

"Ready?" Emilie asked.

Scout gripped the seat backs tightly. "Ready."

She braced herself, remembering the feeling of lifting off from Amatheon's surface, but the moon did not hold them anywhere near so tightly. Emilie, bottom lip firmly between her teeth, fired the rocket in a single short blast. The ground came up under Scout's feet, and for one magical moment, she was standing properly again.

Light from Amatheon flooded the cabin as they rose higher than the mountain range that had been shading them for so many days. The light passed over them in a bright band, then they were beyond that as well, once more in darkness save for the lights of the ship's control panels around them.

The dogs whimpered, and Scout felt herself flinching. As much as she knew better, her instincts were still telling her that making any sound was going to draw attention. But no one could hear them, even if they all screamed at once at the top of their voices.

Sound wasn't what was going to give them away.

"Something in range," Geeta said, using her ensign voice.

Emilie didn't respond, eyes on a digital counter in the console in front of her. When it finally reached zero, she killed the engine. The feeling of standing up drifted away again as the ship maintained its velocity.

"Where are they?" Scout asked, leaning over Geeta's seat.

"Three formations," Geeta said, pointing to the screen. "Following the same basic path as the others."

"Aren't we also heading that way?" Scout asked.

"More or less," Emilie conceded. "But we'll be passing behind them. They won't notice us."

Scout's fingers dug into the spongy material of the seat backs and she leaned forward, trying to catch a glimpse of the ships in the black before them, but without a ship's computer to highlight them, they were invisible.

"We can't see them," Emilie said as if reading her mind. "They can't see us. We only know where they are because their transponders are on. Ours isn't."

"Okay, now we have two more squadrons," Geeta said. "Following the planetary path."

"Does that cross our path?" Scout asked.

"We're going to pass between them," Emilie said. "Neither has any reason to be scanning for us, and without actively looking, they'll never see us. It's okay, Scout. Space is really big."

Scout didn't say anything. It was too strange, the idea that it was possible to hide in the open with no cover. Out on the prairie, it might be possible to duck down into the grass to be out of sight, but anything taller than the grass, any rover or girl on a bike, was visible for kilometers. Even without the plume of dust kicked up by her bike tires.

"Just think, when we get there we'll be able to stand up," Emilie said. "To stretch and jump and run and lie down in a way that actually feels like lying down."

Scout smiled wistfully at that last one. Sleeping in a floating hammock was nice in a way, but it would be nice to sleep without startling herself awake by her own stray hand floating in front of her face like it was someone else about to attack her.

"This is our closest point to the first group," Geeta said, voice at a whisper. Scout strained again to look out the windscreen. She thought she saw three specks together, the edge of one muting a star ever so slightly, but then she might have been imagining it.

"No change," Geeta said. Even her confident ensign voice was betraying a touch of relief.

"I told you," Emilie said, her attention on another counter, one with nearly an hour left to count down.

"Second group, to our left," Geeta said, and she and Scout both looked that way. Geeta glanced back down at the screen from time to time as if to remind herself of their relative positions, but Scout saw nothing out there.

"And they're past," Geeta said, sitting back with a grin. "Now we just wait."

"Yeah, but keep an eye on the screen still though," Emilie said. "We're at the edge of what we've been observing all those days back on the moon. This is probably empty space since the few stations around here are all abandoned, but then again, it might not be. And whatever patrols move through here, we don't know their patterns."

"Shouldn't we have thought of this before?" Scout asked. "There must have been something we could have sent to recon."

"There wasn't," Emilie said. "The ship's computer and I discussed it. But don't worry."

"Space is big," Scout said, and Emilie gave her a thumbs-up.

Scout thought about letting the dogs out, but decided against it. She would just have to stuff them back in the cabinet again before they started the final navigation to the station, and she wouldn't catch them unprepared this time. Besides, they seemed completely content. Gert, for one, seemed to enjoy having Shadow pressed up against her, unable to flee as she nipped at his ears and snuggled against his neck. He occasionally made grumpy sounds of protest, but Scout suspected he didn't hate the attention as much as he pretended to.

"Ships coming," Geeta said, and Scout leaned over her shoulder to see the screen.

It was a bit of an understatement. The edge of the screen was lighting up with more and more dots of light. Dozens and dozens of them, none of them seeming to fly in any sort of formation.

"Are you sure this place is abandoned?" Scout asked.

"Yes," Emilie said, but the way she lingered over the word implied quite a bit less than her usual confidence. "The station isn't even in range yet. Those ships are between us and it, I'm sure of it."

"That's not exactly heartening at the moment," Geeta said to Emilie.

"It's fine," Emilie said. "They still would have to be looking for us to see us. And why would they?"

"Unless we hit one of them," Geeta said. "I think they'd notice that."

"Not likely," Emilie said.

"It's not like you knew they were out here when you did the math," Geeta said.

"The odds of hitting anything are extremely remote," Emilie said.

"Space is big," Scout said again.

"And if something really does look like it's going to get in our way, I'll just goose the positional rockets."

"That will draw attention," Geeta said.

"Maybe, but I don't think it's going to come up."

"I guess we'll see," Geeta said, turning her attention back to the screen.

Scout felt herself getting lightheaded and realized she was holding her breath. She exhaled with a whoosh and Geeta reached back, eyes never leaving the screen, to give her hand a squeeze.

Emilie's lip was back between her teeth, even though she wasn't doing anything with her hands. She was sitting at the controls, but there was nothing she could do but wait, the same as Geeta and Scout.

They were all nervous.

New dots of light finally stopped appearing at the edge of the screen. There was empty space once more, on the far side of what looked like a band of dots all moving past each other, although from where to where wasn't clear. They just had to get past it, like crossing a river.

Not something Scout had ever done, she admitted to herself with a little shiver. The prairie lands she grew up on had mainly been dry. The one river she had seen had by default become one of the borders of the world she inhabited. She wasn't willing to risk trying to cross it with her bike, not when she couldn't see how deep it was, how swift the current was, or what lurked in its muddy depths.

At the moment, she'd rather risk crossing that river.

"Here we go," Geeta said as the band of dots moved down to the center of the screen.

Scout looked out the windscreen in front of them first, then detached the band to float to the back of the cabin to peer at the viewscreens there. Still no sign of anything, although she stared so hard she started seeing stars that weren't out there in the sky.

"Space is big," Emilie said again in a singsong.

"How can they all travel this close together without hitting each other if no one can see each other?" Scout asked, floating back up to the front of the ship.

"All the ships have transponders," Emilie said. "That's why they appear on our scopes."

"But we don't appear on theirs," Scout said.

"Not at the moment, no," Emilie said.

"So they can avoid each other, but they don't even know we're here?"

"Exactly," Emilie said. "The ship will warn us in plenty of time if something is on a trajectory that will cross ours."

"Then we fire our rockets and light up everyone's screens," Geeta said glumly.

"Not likely," Emilie said.

"Which part?" Scout asked.

"Both," Emilie said. "Even if we goose the positional rockets—and it would only take a nudge to get us clear—no one is going to see unless, again, they are actively looking."

"Which they aren't, because if every ship is on scope with its transponder signaling, there's no reason to be looking for anything," Scout said.

"Now you're getting it." Emilie looked back over her shoulder to give Scout that wide, maniacal grin of hers.

It took several long moments to cross the river of ships, but as Emilie predicted, nothing ever passed close enough to them to require evasive action. Scout and Geeta watched the screen as the band of dots moved further and further down the screen, until it vanished completely, dot by dot.

"I just had a thought," Scout said, and Emilie shot her a quizzical look. "What if someone else was out there too, out among the ships, without a transponder signaling? They could be following us, and we'd never know."

"Let's not get paranoid," Emilie said. "We're nearly there."

Scout reattached the tension band to her belt as Emilie's hands hovered over the controls, eyes on the countdown clock. She had put Liam's earpiece in her ear. No one would be guiding her into an unmanned space station; Scout guessed she was listening to the computer talk her through the docking procedure.

"There it is," Geeta said, but she wasn't looking at her screen. She was looking out through the window. Scout's eyes found a patch of darkness that was blotting out stars as the ship drifted forward, more and more stars the closer they got.

"No lights?" Scout said.

"Don't need them," Emilie assured her.

"Protocol says basic life support will be running when we dock," Geeta told her. "It will be cold at first, but there will be air. And once we get to the command deck, we can turn up the heat and turn on all the lights."

"In the meantime, I don't need to see to dock this thing," Emilie said. "The ship does all the work, really."

She put her hands on the controls but still made no moves, just waited with her whole body so tense she reminded Scout of Shadow when he had a mouse trapped in its hole and could hear it scratching around and he just knew it was about to dart out at any moment.

Then Emilie reached forward and pressed a button, one quick jab, and the ship lurched forward and rolled partly on its side.

Not that that meant much when they were once more at a steady velocity and Scout was still floating between the seats. There was no up or down, not yet.

Emilie gave the positional rockets another nudge, changing their trajectory again, and then a third time.

Something was looming over them, not reflecting enough light from distant Amatheon for any of its features to be illuminated. Scout only knew it was big—not as big as the last space station she had been on, not by a long shot, but far more immense than any ship.

Then they were inside, drifting down a long tunnel to the heart of the station. And with the stars now left behind them, they were in complete darkness.

5

THERE WAS some amount of dim light inside the cabin, from the screens and controls strewn across the consoles in front of Emilie and Geeta, but it barely lit up their hands and the lower half of their faces. Everything outside the windscreen was darkness. It felt heavy, oppressive, like some thick black thing that had wrapped itself around their craft.

Anything could be lurking in that darkness, waiting to pounce. Scout tried to swallow down the bitter taste of fear at the back of her throat, but her mouth had gone too dry.

"You can see where you're going, right?" she asked Emilie.

"The ship sees," Emilie said, her hands working the controls. "Hold on tight; I'm stopping our momentum and dropping our magnetic landers. There might be a jolt; this is my first time."

Scout clutched the seat backs and even Geeta, usually so calm, gripped the belts holding her in her seat as if she wasn't sure they would be strong enough.

There was another loud blast from the positional rockets that jerked them all forward. Before Scout had quite gotten back to her place between the seats, the floor dropped sharply away from her, and she heard herself squeal as she nearly lost her grip on the seat backs.

Then she was sitting in a heap on the floor between the two seats, one ankle throbbing from where her foot had taken a wrong turn.

She could scarcely feel that pain, though. It was nothing compared to the joy of being back in gravity, back in a world with an up and a down.

The dogs started yipping, tangled together in the tiny space of the cabinet. Scout unhooked her tension band harness and stumbled to the back to release them as Emilie made some last adjustments on the console and Geeta unbuckled and got to her feet.

"I never appreciated how good gravity feels," Geeta said, interlacing her fingers to stretch her arms up and back, rising to her tiptoes at the apex. She didn't quite smile, but she looked in better spirits than she had since they had boarded Liam's ship.

"What's the plan now?" Scout asked. "Do we stay with the ship in case we need to beat a hasty departure?"

"I don't think that's a bad idea, but it may be excessive," Geeta said. "We should stay near the ship and make sure she's ready to go at any time."

"We should explore the station first," Emilie said. "Make sure we really are alone."

"Who else could be here?" Scout asked. It had looked dark and lifeless when they approached it.

"Other squatters like us," Emilie said.

"Or maybe squatters not so nice as us," Geeta added.

"We should just be sure," Emilie said. Geeta had already gone to the back of the cabin to retrieve her belt and grappler. Emilie pulled her oversized bag of tools from the cabinet next to Geeta's. Scout was already wearing the marshal belt.

She ran her hands over it, taking a quick inventory. Her fingers brushed over the gun loop at the back, empty now. She had been glad to leave the gun behind on Amatheon, but now she wondered if she might regret losing what protection it could offer her. But the few times she had drawn it, had aimed it at others and searched inside herself to find the will to shoot if necessary, she had hated it.

No, she was sure she was better off without it. With no training as to its proper use, it was more danger than help.

"Should the dogs come with us?" Geeta asked.

"They're likely to find trouble before we do," Emilie said, but she looked up at Scout, one eyebrow raised in question.

"They're smart dogs," Scout said. "They can flush out trouble we might miss until it's too late, but they also evade capture pretty handily. We should let them run where their noses guide them."

"Send them out ahead then," Emilie said.

"I would rather it wasn't so dark," Scout said as Emilie reached for the door button.

"It's only dark on the exterior and in the dock," Emilie said. "The ship and I activated the airlock and confirmed the emergency lights are still running within. Low-level light, but better than nothing. Plus, my glasses aren't entirely useless. They do have a few apps that run without the network. Like enhanced night vision."

"I guess I have that too," Scout said, putting her hand in her pocket to touch the single reflective lens that had also once been Gertrude Bauer's. She needed it to use any of the equipment on the belt, but it also had functions all its own.

The door slid open, and the ramp extended, but the dogs hung close to Scout's legs, not eager to be the first ones out in this strange new place.

"Come on, guys. Perfectly safe," Scout said, walking down the ramp. A squarish tent of clear plastic had extended out from the station wall to enclose the area around the ramp, sealing the vacuum out and the atmosphere in. Scout stepped lightly from the end of the ramp to the beginning of the hangar hallway.

The dogs quickly found their bravery and came charging down after her, blowing past her to gallop down the long hallway. Red lights dotted the walls every few meters, spaced far enough apart that the dogs would just disappear into one shadow before appearing in the glow of the next light.

"Do you have schematics for this place or anything?" Scout asked as Emilie came down to stand beside her.

"Not specifically, not yet, but the layout is fixed by the model of station."

"What model is this?" Scout asked.

"They call it a squat torus."

"What does that mean?" Scout asked.

"*Amatheon Orbiter 1* was a cylinder, right? Rotated around its axis to simulate gravity?" Emilie said, and Scout nodded. "A torus is like a wheel, but a thick one, and it rotates around its own axis, too. Because all the stations were originally segments of the *Tajaki 47* hull, that axis is fixed. So this is a torus because it's a much smaller section. Fully staffed, there would only be about a thousand people here, crew and families. Large enough for functioning spin for gravity, though."

"Definitely a plus," Scout said, although truth be told, the bottoms of her feet were already aching, unused as they were to supporting all of her weight. But that would fade away soon enough, Scout was sure, like aching muscles after a hard bike ride.

"Which way to the lights, then?" Scout asked.

"This way. Follow the dogs," Emilie said.

The dogs heard their footsteps and came tearing back, tongues lolling, ears perked with nearly overwhelming excitement. This was a place filled with a plethora of new smells for them to explore, but they wanted to keep their humans near.

Scout glanced back to be sure Geeta was following them. She looked exhausted, but her grappler was in her hands, and she looked ready for anything despite the dark circles under her eyes.

Emilie and the dogs had already started down the hallway. The hallway ended in a large open space, and as they stepped out into the space, Scout saw other corridors running parallel to theirs, all ending in the same room. They must run out to separate landing platforms, Scout guessed. Perhaps once they had the lights on, she could go back out to the ship and see those landing platforms for herself. A thousand people on a station—how many docking stations would they need for travel and supplies? Scout had not a clue.

Emilie paused in the middle of the space and looked around. "They've pulled out a lot of interior features," she said, watching the dogs as they sniffed around the bare metallic floor.

"Like what?"

"Processing stations," Geeta said. "Depending on the threat level, bags and belongings would be inspected on one end, cargo at the other. There should be detectors and partitions and ways to mark off the queues. But that's all gone."

"I guess they took anything that could be reused back to the other stations when they pulled out from here," Emilie said. "To be honest, I thought they'd leave everything in place. This was all supposed to be temporary, right? These stations would be repopulated when our numbers grew."

"That would take decades," Geeta said. "And with the food shortages, the population expansion programs were put on hold."

"But that was supposed to be temporary too," Emilie said. "I've found nothing that says otherwise."

Geeta sighed. "I'm sure everyone hoped it would be temporary, but they planned for the worst-case scenario."

"Does that make it less likely we'll find squatters here?" Scout asked.

"Maybe," Emilie said.

"It means we're unlikely to find supplies left behind. Food and the like," Geeta said.

"We have food enough back at the ship," Scout said.

"And no running water," Geeta said.

They all fell silent at that. Scout suspected she hadn't been the only one looking forward to a hot shower rather than a wipe-down with moist towelettes.

And the dogs, after days in effective diapers, desperately needed baths.

"Lights," Emilie said, looking around once more before choosing a direction: the large opening directly across from all the other hallways leading back to the landing platform. She followed it a short way, then stopped at a door flush with the wall and painted to blend in. Scout wasn't sure how Emilie had even noticed it. She had to pull hard to jerk it open. There was a flicker, then the same low-level red light turned on inside, dully illuminating a steep stairway down.

"I don't think the dogs can handle that," Scout said, frowning at the open grillwork of the metal stairs. "It's so steep it's practically a ladder."

"No need," Emilie said, adjusting her tool bag's strap over her shoulder. "This will just take me a minute."

She clattered down the stairs. Scout looked back to where the dogs were still following scent trails in the receiving area. Geeta alternated between looking backward and forward down the hallway, finger gently tapping the guard over the grappler's trigger.

Then, in a blinding flash, all the lights came on at once. Dimly, from somewhere far deeper within the station, came the sound of music, something slow and melancholy.

"Piece of cake," Emilie said as she emerged at the top of the stairs. "Next step, command deck?"

"Yes," Geeta agreed and led the way further down the hall. Scout gave a whistle, and the dogs bounded to catch up.

The hallway ended in a large open space that reminded Scout of market plazas in the dome cities back on Amatheon, albeit either very early or very late in the day when no one had set up their stalls yet.

She felt a stab of homesickness, which surprised her. She had never liked being inside the cities, not since the day the asteroid had fallen from space and killed her whole family and destroyed her hometown while she was off on a delivery with Shadow. She had avoided cities after that as much as she could, preferring the open prairie.

But the sight of all the white modular building material, the same versatile stuff everything was built with back home, was jarring. There hadn't been a bit of it back on *Amatheon Orbiter 1*. But here it was everywhere, gleaming brightly in the indirect lighting that seemed to flood in from the corners where wall met ceiling.

"Nice," Emilie said. "Why don't we have this back home?"

"We have it on the surface," Scout said.

"I see repeating pieces," Emilie said, trying to look in every direction at once.

"It's modular," Scout said. "There are a certain number of designs, but they all interlock. You can build anything with them. All kinds of shapes. Back home, different neighborhoods had very different design aesthetics, even though the building blocks were the same."

"I'd love to see that," Emilie said.

"For now, the command deck," Geeta said.

"Yes, it's this way," Emilie said and resumed walking.

They were walking down what was effectively a wide road of bare metal like the station hull, with a row of white buildings to either side built of the modular components. The buildings were all empty without a table, chair, counter or broken bottle to testify to having ever been occupied.

But it had been. The white plastic was worn in places where many hands had touched it or feet had passed over it. It was marred with grease or scratches near the doorways, the corners not as sharp as when they had been new. Even without the elements of a planetary system wearing away at it, human activity was enough to take its toll.

"Up here," Emilie said, turning down an alley between two of the white buildings and up an open flight of stairs that led them out of the market area. A bulkhead divided the market area from the rest of the station, but if there was any sort of door to seal it off, Scout saw no sign of it.

Emilie led them down another interior hallway and up another narrower flight of stairs.

The door at the top of the stairs was locked. Geeta stepped forward and took a little device from her belt to place on the door. After a moment, it beeped, and something inside the door clicked. Emilie put a hand on it, and it moved aside easily at her touch.

Scout had expected the command deck to be bigger, but only half a dozen workstations lined the walls. That was all that was needed to manage a station housing a thousand people?

Emilie started at the first of the three workstations on the left, and Geeta moved to the right. Scout hovered uncertainly in the middle of the room, not sure what she could contribute.

"It's actually not all that cold in here," she observed, and Emilie and Geeta both looked up at her. She felt her face flush. "You said the heaters would be off?"

"That *is* odd," Emilie said, exchanging a glance with Geeta.

"No one is here now," Geeta said after tapping through a few screens on the workstation. "I'll run a quick scan, but the last station scan was an hour ago, so I'm sure the only thing it will turn up is us."

"I have the logs here," Emilie said. "People have been squatting here, but all small groups for short periods of time. And no one has been here for days."

"Days?" Scout repeated. She would feel safer if that were a more significant unit of time.

"Yep, just us," Geeta said, turning away from her workstation. "What are we thinking?"

Emilie looked at a few more things on her workstation, then stepped away to join Scout and Geeta in the middle of the room.

"Original plan," Emilie said. "Stay near the ship."

"How will we know if someone is approaching? We need to keep watching the moon too, right?" Scout said.

"I'll stay here," Emilie said. "I can monitor both those things and communicate with the ship from here."

"I'll stay in the ship," Geeta said. She didn't say why, but she didn't have to. She wanted to stay near her sister.

"What about me?" Scout asked.

"Run your dogs around," Emilie said. "Let them get all the exercise they need. They deserve it, and we don't know what's going to happen next."

"Stick close to the ship, though," Geeta said. "Restrict your roaming to between Emilie's position and mine."

"Got it," Scout said.

Emilie nodded and settled herself into her workstation, moving screens around to suit her fancy and settling in for a long watch.

Scout hoped they wouldn't have to wait much longer, but as far as waiting went, this was a much nicer way to do it.

If only she could bathe the dogs.

6

SCOUT STROLLED DOWN the road that was the center of the marketplace for over the hundredth time, hands buried deep in her pockets and eyes on the toes of her canvas high-tops. The dogs had found an interesting smell in one of the buildings. She could hear the sound of them sniffing hard, Gert occasionally whining in her frustration at never finding an actual critter no matter what scent trail she followed.

They had probably found the remains of another squatter camp. About half of the storefronts near the hallway to the hangar showed signs of being camped in. Mostly it was just empty jolo bottles and the scorch marks left behind by ill-advised attempts at building an indoor campfire. Sometimes there were empty trays left behind from long-ago-eaten MREs. Those the dogs ripped to shreds, desperate for any remaining flavor clinging to the biodegradable trays.

Once Scout had found a can of pineapple, completely intact. It had rolled away from the signs of the camp to disappear around a low wall. She had taken that to first Emilie and then Geeta, letting them each have a third of the sweet yellowy goodness.

Liam had left them more food than they would need for months of waiting for his friends to arrive, but nothing sweet. Emilie and Geeta had been as pleased as Scout at her find.

Scout had never tried pineapple before. It tasted like sunshine itself.

The dogs snuffled louder, then got into an altercation over who got to be closer to whatever they were smelling. Scout stepped through the doorway to the building they had disappeared into, not daring to hope there might be another can of pineapple or some other treasure waiting for her.

The dogs had found the tattered remains of a very old bedroll with the combined scent of dozens of unwashed bodies worked deeply into the remaining fabric. Scout could smell it from the doorway and quickly backed away. No wonder the black marketers or whoever had left it behind. The mystery was who could be cold enough in the controlled environment of a space station to turn to such a thing for warmth.

Scout went back to pacing the road. It was better than spending the days floating in the microgravity of the moon, but just barely. Walking was good, but not particularly purposeful, and she needed to have a purpose. She had been working jobs constantly since the age of ten. Having this much time with nothing to do was starting to drive her mad.

And yet, once the Torreses got there, would there be anything for her to do then either? Liam had said the Torreses needed the three of them to testify in court, but he had said that could take years.

She knew testifying meant telling what she knew, describing what she had experienced. That wouldn't take years. No, it would be the waiting again. Over and over again, the waiting. She was going mad just thinking about it.

But she would be in Galactic Central. Surely someone could find something productive for her to do. There must be a million things that needed doing. Sure, most of them would be beyond a backwater planet girl like Scout, and an uneducated one at that. But uneducated or not, she was clever. There had to be something for her to do.

The dogs came charging out of the building for no reason Scout could see, then ran as fast as they could down the road. Shadow was in the lead, as usual, but he banked hard and came back towards Scout.

Gert tried to copy the move and took a tumble. She didn't have his grace or his low center of gravity.

Scout stopped at Gert's side as she rolled back up onto her feet and managed to give her a quick pat on the head before the dog took off again, determined to catch up with Shadow. Scout laughed, then, finding herself at the bottom of the staircase, decided to go up to the command deck to see how Emilie was doing.

Emilie never left the command deck, and Geeta never left Liam's ship. They could speak directly to each other over the comms, but they mostly exchanged greetings and information through Scout. She suspected they were trying to make her feel useful.

"Emilie?" she called softly from the doorway. It was rare, but occasionally Emilie took a catnap in her seat. Scout had woken her once, and as much as Emilie hadn't been mad or even particularly bothered, Scout didn't want to risk doing it again. Emilie surely needed far more sleep than she thought she did.

"Hey, Scout," Emilie said, spinning in her seat to give Scout a grin. "Dogs having fun?"

"As always," Scout said. "Any news?"

"Nothing moving," Emilie said. She had reconfigured the systems on the command deck, displaying all the information she wanted not just on the workstation in front of her but also up on massive screens that loomed down over the two of them. One screen was filled with the image of the moon; indeed, nothing was happening around it. Another showed the vicinity of their station: empty space. She had others monitoring the river of traffic that ran from one of the other space stations to the edge of the barricade and back again.

"I don't suppose Liam ever showed you the process for sending messages through the barricade?" Scout asked.

"No," Emilie said, taking a sip out of a water bulb. Scout looked to the crate in the corner: still half full. No need to bring a resupply from the ship yet. "I think I've worked out the basic principles, but it doesn't do me any good. I could punch through the barricade, maybe, but I don't know where to direct the message. Best not to risk it."

"I suppose not," Scout said, trying not to let her disappointment color her voice. "Did you break into the Space Farer transmissions? I mean," she quickly amended, feeling her cheeks flush again, "your upper management channels." Scout had spent her whole life calling the people who lived up here Space Farers. It was only when she had met Emilie that she learned they didn't call themselves that—and that some of them, like Emilie, detested the term.

"Yeah," Emilie said, tapping a piece tucked into her ear. "No chatter that pertains to us. I think we were chased out by black marketers and those people in black not-quite-uniforms, not anyone from the management of *Amatheon Orbiter 1*."

"So they aren't looking for you?" Scout asked. "Isn't that good news? You could go back."

"I'm not sure there's anything to gain by going back," Emilie said. "Not being chased, I guess, is always a good thing. I've been trying to get news feeds on what happened the day we left—all the fighting and so many people dead—but not a word."

"Is that weird?"

Emilie shrugged. "I can see why it's not in the news feeds that go to all employees. It's obvious why they'd want to keep it a secret. But not telling the other station administrators? That's harder to guess."

The dogs burst into the room in a growling tussle. They had gone back for the filthy blanket and were now engaging in a fierce tug-of-war for it.

"That smells rank," Emilie said.

"What do we do if more squatters come while we're still waiting here?" Scout asked.

Emilie took a moment before answering. "I think most of them, when they see the lights on, will move on without stopping."

"They can see the lights on from outside the station?" Scout asked.

"I'm actually not sure on that. I should probably check. They can certainly see it from the hangar, though. They might dock but then undock and leave the minute they opened their hatch."

"Would you know if someone docked?"

"Certainly," Emilie assured her. The tussle of dogs rolled her way, and she lifted her feet off the floor, letting the tumble of white and black fur pass under her.

"What's that?" Scout asked, squinting up at the center screen above, the one that showed the area around the station.

Emilie frowned and sat forward, examining the same image on the monitor in front of her. "What did you see?" she asked as her eyes scanned for the third time.

"I don't know. Maybe I imagined it," Scout said.

"Describe it anyway," Emilie said.

"A flash? Not really a source of light, more like something reflecting light, but only dully. But there's nothing out there. You'd know if there were, right?"

Scout felt her throat tighten when Emilie didn't answer, just turned her attention to another screen, this one full of data, stacks and stacks of letters and numbers that meant nothing to Scout.

"Maybe you should get the dogs back to the ship," Emilie said.

"What about you?"

"Just a precaution," Emilie said, her voice with that dead quality it had when the words tumbled out of their own accord while her mind was focused intently elsewhere. "I can run if I have to. Maybe this is nothing."

The dogs had stopped play-fighting and were both sitting on the floor, panting loudly and looking up at Scout and Emilie as if they sensed the sudden change in mood.

"Stars!" Emilie cried, stumbling back out of her seat. Scout looked at the monitors in front of Emilie, but they still told her nothing.

Then she looked up at the screen in the front of the room, the one she had seen the flash on before. The image still showed nothing but the blackness of space interrupted by the occasional star, but the station computer was overlaying that image with the outline of ships, each labeled with a blast of data that Scout guessed was being sent from their transponders.

Ship after ship, they just kept appearing, as if an entire fleet had quietly surrounded them, then all switched their transponders on at once.

"How?" Scout gasped.

"We're surrounded," Emilie said. "I don't know how they got so close, but they're all around us."

"Maybe they're from outside the barricade," Scout said. "The tech they have there is so advanced they can probably make themselves invisible to your systems."

"But why would an entire fleet from outside the barricade just show up here, like this? Like they sprung a trap on us?"

"Can you hail them?" Scout asked. "Maybe these are the Torreses?"

"If these are Liam's friends, I'm going to have some words for them about nasty surprises."

She leaned forward to touch the workstation controls, but before her fingertips quite reached the buttons, all the screens went blank at once. Then they all flared back to life, every single one showing the same image of two women, one sitting in a throne-like command chair, fingers curled over the ends of the armrests and legs crossed, and the other standing behind the chair but leaning forward as if to peer over the other's shoulder to get a better look at Emilie and Scout.

"Greetings," the woman in the chair said. "We've been looking for you for a while now. How wonderful to finally see you face-to-face, or nearly."

"Who are you?" Emilie said.

"We are Mai and Jun Tajaki," the woman in the chair answered. "Given the crowd you were running with back at colony ship *Tajaki 47*, you probably know us as the Months."

Emilie gave them a puzzled frown, but Scout knew what the woman was talking about. She and Geeta had told Emilie about the conversation they had overheard when looking for the captive Liam McGillicuddy, but Scout wasn't surprised the detail of that nickname had gotten lost in the sea of other details, especially with Emilie, who always focused more on the technical stuff than the people stuff.

But Scout and Geeta had heard someone refer to the Months. They had been the unseen force directing the black marketers that traded in the hidden corners of *Amatheon Orbiter 1*. They had been trying to exert an influence over the counterculture kids, Emilie's friends. Many of them had died the day Scout and her friends found Liam and made their escape, and Scout would bet whoever had been attacking the kids had really been trying to get at these two and their organization.

But the conversation Scout and Geeta had overheard had been

between two people working for the Months who had been bent on infiltrating the rebellion down on the surface. They had exploited a weak leader, parlaying his trauma at the loss of his wife into a chemical dependency in an attempt to control him.

Scout knew that attempt to control the rebellion for their own aims had failed. She had stumbled over the dead body of the man who had been the go-between, bringing galactic-quality drugs to the rebel leader Malcolm Haley. Without those drugs, he had gone increasingly deranged. He had ordered the rebels to capture Scout, wanting her to divulge information she didn't have. Scout didn't want to think about what he would have done if his own children hadn't turned against him and helped Scout escape.

But what she couldn't afford not to think about was these two women and how far they would go to get what they wanted.

7

THE TWO WOMEN UP on the screen were focusing all their attention on Emilie. Scout took a step back, then another, but no one's eyes tracked her movement. She was unnoticed, for the moment. She looked the women over carefully, searching for any tiny detail that might give her a clue as to who these women really were, deep down inside.

First off, they looked to be in their early twenties, but in Galactic Central, where marshals had body modifications to fight off any kind of disease and most kinds of injury, that might not tell Scout much. They could really be that young, or they could be older than time.

The barricade and the mysterious interference in the Space Farers' world had only appeared since the war, in the last six years. Considering that Amatheon, the surface, and the structures in orbit with all the people contained therein were at the heart of an inheritance dispute, Scout was willing to bet they were actually as young as they looked. The legal battle started as soon as they were old enough to take possession.

It was a theory, anyway.

They dressed alike in black leather pants and low-cut bodices over which they wore long scarlet robes of some shiny, drapey material.

Scout was certain she knew what it would feel like in her hands if she touched it. Gertrude Bauer had worn a white shirt that had looked something like what they were wearing, and holding it had been like touching a shimmering cloud. The Tajaki sisters likely wore something even more delicate. Their dynasty was one of the largest in the galaxy, Scout had been told.

Their hair was long, longer even than their robes, and hung loosely in shimmering waves. Scout resisted the urge to touch her own hair. It was growing out, and what had once been closely shaved was now a chaos of curls with no agreement as to the direction of curling.

She wished she still had her father's bush hat. At least the orange color was starting to fade.

Scout had assumed at first that the Tajaki sisters were twins, like Geeta and her sister Seeta, but then she started to see some subtle differences. The woman in the chair had a more buttony nose, rounder cheeks, and thin, arching eyebrows. The woman behind her had a sharper nose and cheekbones, her eyebrows thicker and straighter, low over her eyes as she scowled. The cosmetics they were wearing looked as if they were attempting to bring both sets of features to a middle ground, as if they wanted people to think they were twins. If they were matching each other's expressions, it might have worked better.

But they would never quite pass for each other, not with those eyes. They were the same deep shade of brown, but while the woman in the chair looked like she was amused by everything that was going on and was willing to indulge Emilie and her suspicions as long as they remained amusing, the one standing behind the chair had something else going on within her eyes. Something wild and dangerous, dormant now but clearly waiting to spring to life at the first perceived provocation.

Scout swallowed hard. There'd been something similar in Malcolm's eyes. But Scout had only ever seen him when he was coming down from the drug he had grown all too dependent on.

What was going on with this woman?

"You have heard of us?" the woman in the chair asked when Emilie failed to respond. She gave a little frown, like a stage gesture.

"I've only heard you mentioned once, and that was secondhand,"

Emilie said. So she had remembered what Scout and Geeta had told her. "I, of course, have no way of verifying that you are who you say you are."

"You must be Emilie Tonnelier," the one in the chair said. "My dear Emilie, who else could we be?"

"Which one are you?" Emilie asked.

"I'm Mai. My sister is Jun," she said. Jun said nothing.

"And you've been looking for us?" Emilie asked. "Who are we, exactly?"

"You and Geeta and Seeta Malini were all ensigns working for the Tajaki colonization division up until the day you left colony ship *Tajaki 47*, although I acknowledge you now refer to it as the *Amatheon Orbiter 1*." Scout took another half step back. They didn't seem to be aware of her at all. They didn't even mention her. Was that a good thing or a bad thing?

"So you're saying we're your employees?" Emilie asked, folding her arms over her chest.

"You're employees of the colonization division, which is a holding of the Tajaki trade dynasty," Mai said.

Scout noted that it wasn't a "yes."

"I understand it is a holding under contention," Emilie said.

"You are, of course, correct," Mai said. "You've been approached to speak on that matter, haven't you?"

"Yes," Emilie said. "But not until after we left *Amatheon Orbiter 1*."

"Interesting," Mai said, giving a brief glance back over her shoulder to her sister Jun. "Perhaps not relevant," she added, turning her attention back to Emilie.

Scout looked down at the dogs, holding her hand palm out to them, fingers spread wide. They knew the gesture, or at least Shadow did. It meant to stay still, stay quiet. Shadow sat in rigid attention, but Gert, bored with the lack of play, flopped down to nap until things got more interesting.

"How could it not be relevant?" Emilie was saying. "You said you've been looking for us since we fled *Amatheon Orbiter 1*, but no one had approached us yet about the legal matter. So why were you looking for us?"

"I understand why you feel distrustful," Mai said with something that didn't quite approach real empathy. "You were swept up in a series of events as you left your home behind, events outside of your control. But you do know we didn't start them. We were the ones in control at the end, but we didn't start any of it."

"The outbreak of violence? It seems not," Emilie said.

"I assure you, once you know us, you'll see that's not our style." Mai looked up at her sister Jun, who made a grimace that Scout was very afraid was meant to be a smile.

"Do you know who did?" Emilie asked. "I lost a lot of friends that day."

"I know—our condolences," Mai said. "The friends you lost were all people of importance to us as well. We feel their loss, if not as deeply."

"Do you know who started the violence?" Emilie asked again.

"Yes," she said. "We are working to bring those people to justice. That's why we are here. We need your help. You were witnesses."

"We were already on our way to testify," Emilie said. Her head made a little twitch, as if she had been about to look back at Scout, but then thought better of it. So she too suspected the Months hadn't noticed Scout there. Scout wasn't sure how that could come in handy, but they weren't in a position to squander any potential advantage.

"Were you?" Mai said with a smile.

"I suspect you know we were," Emilie said, her voice gaining an edge.

"You are, once again, quite correct," Mai said. "You are so very astute. I wish I had found you before you were forced to flee. I could have found so many uses for you."

"I don't like being used," Emilie said.

"Come now, Emilie, you know that's not what I meant," Mai said with the air of a schoolteacher reproaching a student. "You have such skills. Those skills are pointless if you don't put them to some use, aren't they?"

Emilie shrugged.

"To your point," Mai said, uncrossing and then recrossing her legs and shifting to lean on the opposite arm of her chair. "We do know you're waiting here to be picked up by a third party who is attempting to meddle in our legal affairs. Not just the legal affairs of Jun and I, you understand, but of the entire Tajaki trade dynasty. I have no reason to believe you know exactly what that means, except that you strike me as someone who knows all sorts of things she should have no way of knowing."

"I get that your family is super powerful," Emilie said.

Mai smiled brightly. "Yes, we are. And we don't tolerate meddlers. And these meddlers have no power at all. Not a bit. Not even, shall we say, a smidge. They've been caught up on the other side of the tribunal enforcers' barricade. They are never going to get past it, I'm afraid. They can keep trying to file motions, but really they are as the buzzing of a gnat to our army of lawyers." Then she paused, her smile wavering. "I'm sorry. I quite forgot that you grew up in space. A gnat is—"

"I know what a gnat is," Emilie said.

"Of course," Mai said, summoning up that smile once more. "So I hope you can see that we're really here to rescue you. I'm sure you realize the people who instigated the violence back at your home are still looking for you. It's only a matter of time before they find you. Clever as you are."

"And the people who instigated the violence are...?" Emilie prompted.

"Really, it would be far more comfortable to tell this long, tragic story over a meal," Mai said. "You will be our guests."

"Guests," Emilie repeated dubiously.

"Of course," Mai said. "I'm not offended that you don't trust us. Trust has to be earned. I promise you we will earn it. But for now, know that we are here on this side of the barricade with the blessing of the tribunal enforcers and that a ménage of them is with us now. They will always be there when the two of us and the three of you are in the same room, to observe. We cannot coerce you; they will not allow it. I do hope we can persuade you to help us, however."

She smiled again, but Scout felt an icy chill run up her spine. Three of you, she had said. Did that mean Emilie, Geeta, and Seeta? Or did it mean Emilie, Geeta, and Scout?

"I need to talk to Geeta about it first," Scout said.

"Of course," Mai said brightly. "She is on the marshal's ship, and she's heard this entire conversation from there. You go to her and talk it over, and when you're ready, just float out of the dock and we will pick you up. The ship will stay in our hangar until you require it again. I promise you,"—she leaned forward, elbows on her knees and hands clasped together—"*promise* you that you will be free to leave any time you wish."

Emilie just nodded and then turned her back on the screen. The image of the sisters winked out, replaced by the previous image of the computer-labeled fleet of ships. For a moment, they were still all but invisible against the black, but in the blink of an eye, they all turned on their exterior lights. Many were so small and so far away they were just dots, barely brighter than the stars behind them, but others were larger and closer. But none of them could catch Scout's attention once her eyes fell on the central ship of the fleet.

It was massive, larger than the space station they were standing in. It gleamed like chrome, just as Liam's ship did, but where his ship was fine as a needle, this was hulking, like a bird of prey with a thick central body flanked by two immense arms that thrust forward. It was like that ship was reaching for them, ready to tear the station apart to get at them.

Scout didn't realize she had gasped out loud until Emilie stopped in the doorway to look back, first at Scout and then at the screen. But she seemed unmoved.

"Come on," she said, and Scout summoned the dogs to follow her as she ran to catch up with Emilie. They didn't speak as they jogged back through the empty marketplace and across the hangar to where Liam's ship was docked.

Geeta was waiting for them just inside the door of Liam's ship. Her face was grim.

"The people who started the fighting must be the other half of the Tajaki dynasty," she said.

"I was thinking the same," Emilie agreed.

"They seem more on our side than the others," Scout said. She was picturing the woman dressed all in black, the woman who had more advanced body modifications even than Liam, the woman who had flung Seeta out of the station hangar and into the vacuum of space.

Liam had caught her body, but it was still to be seen whether Seeta could be revived from the stasis he had put her in or if they were too late.

A look of pain and sorrow tightened Geeta's features, and Scout knew she was picturing the same woman. Going with the Months might be a way to strike back at that woman, somehow.

But, apparently, Geeta had come to a different conclusion. "The lesser of two evils is still evil," she said.

Emilie nodded and slipped into the pilot's chair. "The ship and I have come up with a few options. I don't have time to explain, but..."

She didn't need to. Geeta grabbed Gert, and Scout scooped up Shadow, and they tucked the dogs back inside their little cupboard. By the time they had strapped themselves in, Emilie had closed the ship's door and unmoored them from the dock.

And once more, they found themselves pushing forward into impenetrable darkness.

8

EMILIE DIDN'T TURN them around to go back the way they had entered from, just let the ship drift out to the center of the open space within the station. Scout figured, as this station was a section of the *Tajaki 47* hull just like *Amatheon Orbiter 1,* only smaller, they could exit from either end.

But the station was surrounded. The Months were probably on that immense flagship waiting for them on the side facing the moon, but other ships would be watching for them if they emerged from the other end, wouldn't they?

"How are we going to sneak past?" Geeta asked.

"We're not going to," Emilie said and flashed them both that maniacal grin before sliding the accelerator lever as far forward as it would go.

Scout lost her hold on the seats and fell back, stretching the tension band that was her tether to the max. She grasped it with her hands to reel herself back in and tried not to panic at how hot the rubbery plastic was under her palms. If it snapped, she'd hit the back wall of the ship and likely break every bone in her body.

Geeta was pressed flat back against her seat but still managed to turn her body and extend an arm to Scout. Scout took it and crawled just a bit closer, then felt Geeta's other hand on her back, guiding her to sit on the floor between Geeta's legs. That did seem the safest option, although by the time Scout had battled the continuing acceleration to reach that safety, she was drenched in sweat, her arms and legs shaking from the effort.

And she couldn't see what was going on.

"Hold on," Emilie said from between gritted teeth, and Geeta grasped both of Scout's shoulders as Emilie pounded at something on the console.

It was like the ship had hit a wall, and only Geeta's firm hold on Scout's shoulders kept her from knocking herself out against the console in front of her. That stopped their forward momentum, but it was instantly replaced by a sideways acceleration. Scout flailed about, trying to find a handhold before she started tumbling away. Geeta thrust a foot against the console, making a barrier of her leg that kept Scout in place.

Scout was instantly very, very happy that Geeta had been dealing with her grief by exercising. Those muscles were all that stood between her, with her still-trembling limbs, and a nasty head wound.

"That took them by surprise," Emilie said.

"They'll pursue," Geeta said. "This ship is fast, but they likely have faster. A lot of their ships look light, built for speed."

"Maybe," Emilie said, "but those same fast ships likely aren't built for atmosphere."

"Atmosphere?" Scout said, suddenly desperate to see where Emilie was taking them. She clamored up from the floor and Geeta helped her sit on the edge of the seat in front of her, finally able to see out of the windscreen. Geeta's arms tightened around her middle in case Emilie decided to change their velocity again in a hurry.

"Atmosphere," Emilie said with a grin at the same moment the ship began to rattle around them.

"This didn't happen when we took off," Scout said, shouting over the building noise. "Are you sure you're doing this right?"

"The ship says we're within tolerances," Emilie said. Wisps were starting to streak past the windscreen, so faint against the star field beyond they almost seemed imaginary, but the bucking ship beneath them swore they were real.

"Emilie?" Geeta said. Not panicked, just prompting her for more information.

"We have to push it hard. We have to lose as much of our tail as we can. The ship can take it," Emilie said, each word popping out as a separate declaration as the majority of her mind focused on flying.

"Where are we going?" Scout asked.

"You think. In a minute. I have to… hold on," she said, pounding something else on the console. The ship rolled, and they were falling upside down, then spiraling around sickeningly until they were diving headfirst.

Scout heard her dogs whimper and knew that last maneuver had at least bruised them, if not worse. Geeta, who had all but screamed with the effort to hold onto Scout when they were upside down, now fought to breathe as all of Scout's weight pressed back against her, but there was nothing Scout could do—because they were still accelerating at a rate that had her pinned down on top of Geeta with a force several times normal gravity, and because the sight of the planet's surface rushing up to meet them, growing ever larger and more detailed through the windscreen, had paralyzed her with fear.

"Hold. On." For a moment, Scout feared the acceleration was too much for Emilie, that she wouldn't be able to raise her arms even the short distance she needed to in order to reach the console.

But Emilie's groan of effort morphed into a yell of triumph, and she pulled the ship out of its death dive.

And then they were gliding smoothly along through a blue sky dotted with little puffs of clouds.

"Lost them, I think," Emilie said. "Give it a minute."

"We can't do that again," Geeta said.

Scout slid to the front of the seat, then got up to lean forward, peering through the very bottom edge of the windscreen.

"No, we can't," Emilie agreed. "Not enough altitude now."

"I don't know where we are," Scout said. The Amatheon she had known had been red-gold prairies of grain, hills sparsely covered by gray-green vegetation, barren mountains, and the occasional brightly colored canyon. What was below her was an expanse of blue waves ending in a whitish-gray beach, then darker gray cliffs of bare rock, then an endless forest of shady green trees.

"Don't worry about it," Emilie said. "The ship logged where Liam picked you up. We can go back there, or anywhere near there you think is safe."

"The rebels are near there," Scout said.

"I thought you said they were bad news," Geeta said.

"Yeah," Scout said. "But that was because they were being manipulated by these sisters, the Months. If we told them all we know, I suspect we'd have some allies."

"Allies with more power than we have right now," Geeta said.

"We could use allies like those," Emilie said. "I'm going to circle in that direction, though, not fly straight there. If the Months are manipulating the rebels, they must know where they are. We might have to land further out and sneak in."

"There are a few villages close by," Scout said. "We could get supplies. Everything in this ship is worth a fortune down there."

"Good to have options," Emilie said, then yawned widely. She grinned at the other two. "That was exhausting."

"We're not done yet," Geeta said, looking worried.

"No, I'm good," Emilie said. "I'm going to circle back and check our tail. Delicately this time, I think."

The ship traced a spiral, dropping lower as it banked around until they were facing the direction they had come. Scout's eyes were up, searching the skies for signs of pursuers, although she knew the ship was certain to detect more than she could see with her naked eyes.

The sky was a breathtaking shade of indigo. Over the prairie, the sky was usually a more washed-out shade of blue, as if someone had mixed the clouds and sky together into one uniform grayish blue. But she had seen a sky like this before: the day she had left her family, never to see them again.

"Stars," Geeta gasped, and Scout looked to see what had caught her attention. She wasn't looking up at the sky, wasn't looking for pursuers at all. She was looking down at the waves of water below them. The ship was low enough now for them to see the whitecaps as the waves curled before rushing up to the shore. "It's more than I ever imagined. And to think you grew up here."

"I only saw the ocean one time, and it was from shore," Scout said. "Still, it's mind-blowing, isn't it? All that water. It makes you wonder what all is hidden beneath it."

"We're going to cross it now," Emilie said. "Liam picked you up on the other side of the planet."

"How long?" Scout asked.

"To get there? Maybe an hour. I want to go slow, keep scanning for trouble. Plus, I'm starving."

"I'll get you something," Scout said, heading to the back of the ship. She came back with a couple of protein bars for Emilie, nothing that would be messy if she had to drop it in a hurry. Then she went back to check on her dogs.

They both had their noses pressed through the open mesh of the tape enclosure. Scout put her hand on each nose so they could smell her and know she was okay. She didn't want to let them out in case Emilie had to start making evasive maneuvers again, but she did risk detaching one corner to reach inside and scratch around their ears.

"You guys okay?" she asked.

Gert made no sound, just turned to push her nose into the scruff of Shadow's neck. Shadow whimpered.

"Are they okay?" Emilie asked, turning in her seat to look back at Scout with a look of deep worry.

"I think so," Scout said, running her hands over Shadow's little body. "Nothing broken. Maybe a little battered, though."

"We can take a better look after we land," Geeta promised. "We still have the med kit if we need it."

Scout longed to take Shadow out of the cabinet and hold him on her lap. Gert liked being near her, but Shadow had a deep, visceral need to be touching her, and she was sure that, hurt as he was, he was feeling that need more powerfully than ever.

But it wouldn't be safe.

"Gert, take care of our boy for me, okay?" Scout said.

Gert nosed Scout's hand, then bent to gently nip at Shadow's ears.

Shadow sighed but accepted her attention as a weak substitute for Scout's.

The first sign that they were reaching the end of the ocean was the bright gleam of a dome magnifying the setting sun behind it. The capital city. Scout had only been there a few times. It overlooked the ocean, but she had always been on the land side of the city, except for the one time she had gone down to the shore just to see the water.

Beyond the capital were kilometers of green fields, some sort of low, leafy plants Scout couldn't identify. But soon enough the lush soil gave way to the sparser, drier ground of the prairie and the squares of green became an endless expanse of red-gold, the heavy heads of grain dancing and bowing in the breeze.

Home. It felt strange to be back. She had never intended to come back, certainly not so soon. At least she had friends with her this time.

"No need to go back to the pickup spot," Scout said. "It's pretty remote."

"Gotcha," Emilie said and called up a map onto the console screen. "Where?"

Scout leaned in to study the map. "There, that band of color. That's the canyon where the rebels are hiding."

"Wow," Geeta said. "Such colors."

"It's even more impressive up close," Scout said. "You'll see."

"I will," Geeta said, as if just realizing that was true. She broke into a genuine smile, and Scout caught her hand and gave it a squeeze.

"No sign of pursuit," Emilie said. "I'll circle around one more time, and then we'll land there, at the mouth of the canyon."

The ship made another lazy spiral, this one in a large but complete circle. When they were once more facing west, they were even closer to the ground than before, so close Scout felt like if she opened the door and leaned out, she could touch the tops of the stalks of grain.

She was going to have to find a way to speak to Joelle first. Joelle understood about her father and would be the most receptive to what Scout had to tell her about how he had been manipulated. Her brother Reggie would listen too, but since he was only twelve and seldom allowed to leave the hideout, she was unlikely to encounter him first.

It might be one of the mechanics—motormouth Ken or laconic

Bente—out on patrol on their motorcycles. They often worked as a team. She might have to talk a bit faster with those two, but in the end, they would at least let her make her case to Joelle or Bente's uncle Arvid. With Malcolm laid up, Arvid would be the one calling the shots.

Scout had no sense of Arvid. Her experience with him was too limited. But with the others to speak on her behalf, and with what she had to tell, she could surely get him to listen. He had been far more stable than Malcolm.

That left only Tucker.

She didn't want to think about Tucker.

Ironically, he would probably be the easiest of the rebels to win over. He would do anything for her, or so he said. But he had said that before, and then he had betrayed her. Saying it again now and swearing anything was worth it if she gave him one more chance didn't make it any more believable to Scout.

Even if he were completely sincere, Scout didn't see any good coming from using him to get inside. She was still too angry that he had betrayed her, too angry that he had nearly killed her dogs by shooting them with a tranquilizer he had no idea how to properly cali-brate to their respective sizes. Just thinking about Tucker was making her curl her hands into fists. What would happen if she actually saw him again?

"This is it," Emilie said, and Scout forced her hands to uncurl, her teeth to stop biting her lip, and her head to rise so she could look out the windscreen at the canyon opening. The walls here were a bland dusty yellow, but deeper in, they would be like a dazzling rainbow created by trace minerals in the rock.

Emilie set the ship gently down and turned off the engines.

"Look," Geeta said, leaning forward to point through the wind-screen. A faint plume of dust was rising up from deeper within the hills. "Someone is coming?"

"They would have seen us approaching," Scout said, and swal-lowed hard. "Maybe I should go out alone."

"Together," Emilie said and unbuckled her harness.

She had just climbed out of the seat, eyes on Scout as she prepared to argue with any objections Scout might have, but they both turned at Geeta's startled gasp.

Two ships set down on the ground between them and the canyon mouth. They were two of the lighter fliers, only room for one pilot each. The ships were close enough for them to see those pilots through their windscreens.

They didn't look happy.

"We can fight them," Geeta said.

"No, we run," Emilie said, jumping back into the pilot seat.

"No, I agree with Geeta," Scout said. "There are only two, and the rebels are on their way. This might be our only chance."

Before Emilie could answer, the ship under them began to shake. Then the ground started falling away beneath them. They were rising up into the air, and their engines weren't even on yet.

Scout had one glimpse of a pair of motorcycles emerging from the canyon, skidding to a halt to gape up at the sky. Scout was pretty sure it was Ken and Bente.

Then metallic walls dropped down around the sides of the ship, or rather the ship rose up into them, and every glimpse of her home world was gone.

9

SCOUT TIPPED her head back to look up, hoping for a glimpse of whatever they were rising up into, but the lights above them were blindingly bright. The only detail she could see was the square of metal walls around them.

A hull, she realized. They kept rising and rising, but the metal before them wasn't made of separate sections welded together. It was solid, the space they were in neatly carved out of it. Whatever had carved it out had left patterns on the metal like overlapping fans. They were shaped like a fan you'd hold in your hand to keep the heat off on a sweltering day, but they were immense, wider than Scout could spread her arms.

"Stars," Geeta said, her voice barely more than an awed whisper. "The hull is so thick. What was this ship built for?"

"How is it staying aloft?" Emilie wondered, peering up into the light above them. Her glasses darkened to compensate. "It must be incalculably heavy, and they brought it this far down a gravity well."

"It's the big one, isn't it?" Scout said.

"The flagship? Makes sense," Emilie said. "Is this common tech in Galactic Central? I can't wait to get there."

"Well, I guess they're planning on taking you over," Scout said miserably. "So you'll get to see it."

"Us," Geeta said. "They said all three of us." Scout didn't know what to say, but apparently, Geeta saw it in her eyes, anyway. Her gaze dropped to the panel under Scout's feet, the panel that covered the small space where her sister lay in protective stasis. "Oh."

"You're not getting left behind," Emilie said. "I don't care what they were thinking, how they grouped us into three. Four of us are going, or none of us are."

Scout nodded glumly. She didn't see how they had any way of negotiating for anything.

The brightness above became a brightness all around them, and Scout had to shade her eyes and turn away. A moment later she risked a peek and saw that the light was dimming once more as they rose up out of the end of the tunnel through the hull and hovered in the air for a moment as a hatch closed beneath them. Then whatever had picked them up set them gently down on top of the hatch.

They were in a hangar, a scattering of ships all around them: mostly lightweight craft like those which had headed them off at the mouth of the canyon but a few larger shuttles and even another sleek, needle-shaped ship like the one they were in.

Something underneath them clanged as it clamped onto them, and they were moving, off of the top of the hatch to a position among the other parked vehicles.

There was still no sign of people out in that hangar, just ships.

"How mad do you think they're going to be?" Scout wondered.

"The one in the chair I suspect is going to respect us for the attempt," Geeta said as she got up from her seat and went to the back to fetch her belt and grappler. "The one behind the chair? She looks like she'd consider it an insult."

"She'll be livid," Emilie said, drawing out that last word.

"I guess we find out how well her sister has her in check," Geeta said, checking the indicator on her grappler before hooking it onto her belt.

"You think they'll let you keep that?" Scout asked.

"We'll see," Geeta said.

"Listen, with that counting of three," Scout said. "If they mean the three of us and don't know we have your sister, what then?"

"What do you mean?" Geeta asked with a frown.

"They might not know we caught her," Scout said. "They might think she was lost when she tumbled out of the hangar bay."

"Oh," Emilie said. "It might be better to keep her hidden. I agree."

"She's safe in stasis where she is," Scout said to the still-frowning Geeta. "But if they know she's here, they might try to use her for leverage."

"Or worse," Emilie said.

Geeta stared at a spot on the floor for a long moment, then gave a sharp nod. She didn't seem to trust herself to speak.

Gert made a squeak, the little sound she made when she was widely yawning. And she yawned widely when she was feeling stressed and unsure. Scout bent to peel back the mesh of tape, noting briefly that it was far too battered to be much good if they did try to fly out of here again in the future, then reached in and picked up Shadow.

He was trembling, but the moment she had him in her arms, he squirmed against her to press his face tight against the side of her neck. Scout felt tears prick at her eyes but blinked them away. He would be okay; he just needed a little comfort. She stroked the hair on his back and murmured nonsense close to his ear.

Emilie, tool bag already slung across her body, bent down on one knee and held out her hands to Gert, who emerged from the cabinet. Her entire back end was pivoting back and forth, propelling that white-tipped tail in an ecstatic wave as she rushed up to her second-favorite human.

There was a sudden knock on the side of the ship, someone rapping on the part of the hull that would drop down to form a ramp. Geeta went to the windscreen to peer out but shook her head; no one was visible.

"Let's put her on a leash first," Scout said, reaching for the cabinet where she had stowed the cord leashes she had made for both dogs when she had first taken them up into space. "Can you keep her close to you?"

"Of course," Emilie said, taking one of the cords from Scout's hand

and deftly tying it around Gert's worn collar. Gert just pressed herself up against Emilie's calf, clearly communicating her willingness to stay close at her side. Geeta helped Scout tie the other cord to Shadow's collar, just in case. Then Emilie pushed the button to open the door and lower the ramp.

Scout wasn't sure what she had expected to see waiting for them on the deck below. A phalanx of guards, guns drawn, perhaps? Certainly not the Months themselves, although that image suddenly seemed more plausible than the one that greeted them now.

A solitary figure moved forward to stand at the bottom of the ramp, a man of advanced years with a frizz of sparse white hair floating around his wrinkled black scalp. He smiled up at them, clasping his hands together as he saw the three of them looking back down at him. His eyes went from Geeta to Emilie and then to Scout, and for a flash, Scout felt like there was something familiar about those brown eyes. But then he looked back to Geeta, and Scout gave her head a little shake.

She had never met this man before; she was sure of it. And yet he felt familiar.

"Greetings," he said, giving his clasped hands a little shake. "The Months are waiting to receive you. If you'll follow me?"

"Do we have to?" Emilie asked.

He seemed surprised at the question. "No, you don't have to. But dinner is about to be served, and they'd like to have a word with you first. If you prefer, food can be brought to you here. You are our guests."

Emilie scoffed.

"We should just go," Geeta said. "I'd rather see this through than keep hiding on this ship." She wrinkled her nose, and Scout realized that while she and Emilie had been on board the station, Geeta had remained behind in the ship that never quite didn't smell of dog urine.

"Yes, let's go," Scout said, leading the way down the ramp. Shadow burrowed deeper against her neck and whimpered but didn't attempt to jump away from her. Geeta followed behind her, Emilie and Gert bringing up the rear.

"You work for the Months?" Emilie asked as they started walking across the hangar.

The man turned to look back at her as he walked and summoned a little smile. "Indeed. I guess you could say I'm their majordomo, if that's not too grand a title. I keep the ship and the Months' court running smoothly so they can focus on other things."

"Do we address you as Majordomo? Or Sir Majordomo or something?" Geeta asked.

"Oh stars, no. Caleb will be fine," he said, looking genuinely appalled.

"I'm guessing you already know who we are," Emilie said.

"Ensign Emilie Tonnelier," Caleb said with a nod. "You would be Ensign Geeta Malini, correct?"

If Geeta had heard the little pause before her name that Scout had, she gave no sign of it, just gave a curt nod.

"And me?" Scout asked.

"You would be Scout Shannon," he said with a warm smile. "We've been watching you for quite some time."

"Watching me?" Scout said.

"Oh yes. I might be speaking out of turn, but the Months find you quite fascinating," he said. "Especially Jun. Although…" He looked around to be sure they were still alone as they crossed the hangar. There was no sign of anyone anywhere, no one prepping a ship to fly or performing maintenance or anything, as if they were in a graveyard for abandoned ships. Even so, he leaned closer to whisper, "You might not be able to tell. Jun is a tough read until you get to know her."

Scout didn't know how to respond to any of that, but then she didn't have to. Emilie was happy to continue grilling the majordomo herself. "You've known her long, then?"

"Six years now," he said.

"I thought you were going to tell us you've known them since they were babies," Emilie said. They had reached the edge of the hangar and Caleb led them down a long, narrow hallway. Like the passage the ship had risen through, everything looked like it had been carved into a single immense piece of metal. There were no joins, no panels or screws or fastenings, save the occasional door. It was like being inside a cave.

A neatly squared-off cave carved from metal. So not really much like a cave at all. Scout adjusted the dog in her arms and took a few rushing steps to catch up with the others.

"Six years," she said as she fell back into step beside Caleb. "When the barricade went up."

"Correct," Caleb said.

"So which side are you from originally?" Scout asked. "Galactic Central or Space Farer?"

Caleb smiled at her indulgently. "'Space Farer'—I haven't heard that term in ages. But that is what I am. A, as you 'Planet Dwellers' say, Space Farer."

"How did one of us end up serving as majordomo for a branch of the Tajaki trade dynasty?" Geeta asked.

Caleb drew to a halt before a pair of tall, closed double doors and turned to face the three of them. "That is a very long tale, one which I'd be happy to share with you at any point in the future. Find me later, absolutely any time, and I'll regale you with so many stories you'll beg me to stop." He smiled again. "But for now, the sisters await. And I don't like to keep them waiting."

"I suppose not," Emilie said, reaching down to give Gert's head a reassuring pat.

Caleb summoned one last smile, this one with a distinct undertone of nervousness to it that made Scout hug Shadow just a bit tighter.

Then he turned to fling open the massive doors—surely too heavy for such a small, frail man; Scout suspected some sort of magical Galactic Central technology at work—and marched into the room beyond.

The center of the room was a single long strip of carpet, scarlet like the cloaks the sisters wore. Caleb walked briskly along this carpet, nodding and waving to the crowds pressing in close on either side to watch the three of them enter the hall. Scout saw someone start to stumble, only to be caught and hauled back by his neighbors before he could accidentally put a foot down on that brilliant carpet.

But the three of them would have to step on it in order to follow

Caleb, who was even then turning to wave at them urgently, summoning them to follow.

Because at the other end of the carpet was a little raised dais, and on that dais was a pair of throne-like chairs. And in those chairs were the Tajaki sisters, also known as the Months. And they were waiting.

10

SCOUT HUGGED Shadow close and stepped out onto that scarlet carpet. Her feet sunk into its lush depth. She could only imagine what it would feel like to walk barefoot across such softness. Even through the soles of her canvas shoes, it was like a delightful massage.

Geeta followed close behind and to the left of Scout, her hands ready on the grappler no one had asked her to leave behind. Emilie had a little trouble convincing Gert to step out onto that strange floor, to walk between two masses of strangers, more people than Gert was used to since she was quite a young puppy living alone on the streets of one of the domed cities. But she trusted Emilie nearly as much as she trusted Scout and finally allowed herself to be led through the double doors.

The crowd had been murmuring amongst themselves when Caleb had thrown the doors open, but they all fell into silence as the three of them crossed the room. A few leaned together to whisper behind cupped hands, but most just watched them walk by. Their chaotic mix of clothing and general attitude reminded Scout of the black market hidden in the depths of *Amatheon Orbiter 1*. In fact, a few looked downright familiar, and she wouldn't be surprised to find they were the same people. If they all worked for the Months, that made sense.

And now they had been summoned to court.

Mai and Jun watched them approach without a word. Mai had a warm smile on her lips, but Jun was fidgeting in her chair, drumming her fingers on the arms and bouncing her knees. Finally, she gave up the attempt to sit still and jumped up to pace the dais behind the two chairs.

Caleb paused for a moment at the bottom of the dais, then bowed and stepped to one side. Scout, not certain if she was meant to follow but very certain she was not about to bow to anybody, stopped with the toes of her blue-with-white-polka-dot sneakers at the very edge of the carpet. Geeta drew up beside her, then Emilie stepped up on Scout's right side. Gert looked up at the two women towering over them and dropped into her lopsided sit, her pelvis rolling so she rested rather indelicately on one hip.

"Welcome," Mai said, spreading her hands as if to encompass the room and everyone in it.

"Okay," Emilie said guardedly.

"Since we picked you up, we've flown out of your planet's atmosphere and are making our way to the barricade gate. Once the tribunal enforcers let us pass, we'll be on our way to Galactic Central, but in the meantime, we do hope you'll join us for a meal."

She indicated a room off to the right with a tilt of her head, but Scout needed no hint as to which direction the food was. The air was thick with smells: fresh-baked bread, sizzling meat, roasted vegetables, caramelized onions. Even Shadow in her arms finally perked up a bit, lifting his head to sniff at the air. Gert was smelling it, too.

"Strings attached?" Emilie said, not exactly a question.

"No strings attached, my dear Emilie," Mai said. Jun made a low growling sound in her throat and ceased her pacing to lean over the back of her sister's chair, but still said not a word. Mai gave her a little glance and then turned back to Emilie. "I'm sure warm, fresh food must be welcome to you. I can't imagine what you were living on in that abandoned station."

Emilie didn't answer, but Mai gave her another smile, like that was exactly what she expected.

Caleb might think that Jun was fascinated with Scout for whatever reason, but Scout suspected that paled in comparison to the regard Mai had for Emilie.

"Well, shall we?" Mai asked, getting up from her chair with a completely superfluous swirl of her scarlet robe.

"Just like that? No questions first?" Emilie asked.

"Aren't you hungry?" Mai asked over her shoulder as she stepped down from the dais and passed through the open doorway to the room beyond. Her sister jogged to catch up with her, her own scarlet robe billowing out behind her a bit less elegantly. Caleb emerged from the edge of the crowd to hurry after them, hands clasped together as always.

Emilie turned to look at Scout and Geeta, her eyebrows raised so high they had disappeared behind the thick whorls of her candy-red hair. "What. The. Heck," she said.

"They're playing with us," Geeta said.

"What do we do?" Scout said.

"I guess we go in and eat," Emilie said, but none of them took a step off the carpet.

The crowds around them were starting to flow through the doorway. Scout could see the end of a long table covered in bowls of food, baskets of bread, and decorative lights that had a warm hue, almost like actual candlelight. It would have to be a long table indeed to seat so many.

"They're not going to make us sit with them or anything?" Geeta said. "This is really weird."

Scout was about to agree when a voice cried out over the din of the moving crowd. "Seeta!"

Geeta flinched, turning away from the crowd before they could see the sharp pain that tightened her features. Emilie stepped up to put a hand on her arm in comfort, but her eyes were scanning the crowd.

Then Scout saw her, the girl of no more than ten she had seen from a distance but never met. She had warm brown skin and hair gathered on top of her head that sprouted out of the ponytail holder like a smooth globe over the top of her head.

What was her name again? Her brother Hal had been a close friend of Seeta's, might have been more than a friend if he hadn't died so suddenly from an assassin's poison dart. The same assassin, in fact, that had pushed Seeta off the hangar deck and out into space.

"Sparrow!" Scout called, finally remembering the girl's name. But the girl who had just stopped in front of them, carefully not on the carpet, looked at her in puzzlement. "You don't know me, but I'm a friend of Seeta's."

"Yeah," Sparrow said, eyebrows furrowed together as she looked from Scout to Geeta, who still wasn't looking at her.

"I'm sorry, I should explain," Scout said. "This is Seeta's sister, Geeta."

"Oh, hi," Sparrow said, brightening. "I remember now. Twins, right?"

"Yes," Geeta said.

"So where's Seeta?" Sparrow asked, looking around as if she might have missed seeing her when the three had made their long progression down the hall.

"She's not here," Scout said carefully, glancing up at Emilie.

"Not here?" Sparrow said.

"Sparrow, I'm so sorry. You do know about your brother, don't you?" Scout asked.

Sparrow's face fell. "Yeah. Some of the others told me. No one caught the woman who did it either."

"I'd like to," Geeta said, one hand tensing into a fist. "I intend to."

"But no one knows who she is," Sparrow said.

"No one? No one here knows?" Emilie asked.

"Yeah. Not even the Months. They are awfully curious about her, though. I think they were hoping you knew?" Her voice trailed off, but Scout gave a sad shake of her head.

"We couldn't catch her, and we don't know who she is," Scout said.

"So where's Seeta?" Sparrow asked again. It was obvious there would be no distracting her from that point.

Scout looked at Emilie and Geeta. She wasn't sure she knew how to craft a convincing lie.

Then, to her surprise, Geeta just blurted out the truth. "That assassin tried to kill her. Nearly succeeded. Seeta is in stasis back on our ship."

"Stasis?" Sparrow repeated, alarmed. "She's alive though?"

Geeta couldn't answer. Emilie gave a little shrug.

"But they can help her here," Sparrow said, clutching at Geeta's arm. "There's a whole hospital in this place. Why did you leave her behind in that dinky little ship?"

"She's safe," Geeta tried to assure her, but Sparrow was already gone, fleeing into the dining hall. The low murmur of voices that had traveled with the crowd as it exited the room was becoming a din of revelry on the other side of that doorway.

"Does she have pull with those two?" Emilie asked as they watched Sparrow run straight up to where the two sisters sat at the head of the table and make some passionate plea, hands pressed together in supplication.

"Maybe you shouldn't have said anything," Scout said. "If they take her to the hospital, they'll put her in a pod or hook her up to a machine or something, and we won't be able to move her. And there is no escape for the three of us without her."

"We won't be escaping," Geeta said stiffly. "Not from this place. It's quite impossible."

"They might use her against you," Scout said, but her voice dropped off as Geeta turned to fix her with an icy stare. "Sorry. You're right. If they can help her, this is what we have to do."

Sparrow came skipping back, Caleb hurrying along behind her, a look of grave concern on his face.

"Why didn't you tell me?" he nearly wailed. "I would have taken her to the hospital immediately, even before taking you to the audience chamber. Oh, I wish you had said something."

"We said something now," Geeta said, her voice still cold.

"I shall see to the transport of your sister at once," he said. "Why don't you join Sparrow at the table? I don't expect you to make merry with the others, but do get some warm food in you. I'll send someone to fetch you the very moment we have your sister stabilized in a medical pod. Please?"

Geeta gave another curt nod, and a look of profound relief washed over his face. He waved them on towards the dining room, waiting for each of them to step off the end of the carpet and follow Sparrow towards the dining hall before finally turning away and jogging back to the hangar.

Shadow started stirring in Scout's arms, excited by the plethora of food smells that filled the room. Sparrow led them to an open spot further down the table, then reached for bowl after bowl, filling their plates with great heaps of steaming food with impressive speed. She even prepared two smaller plates with slices of meat and set them on the ground for the dogs. Shadow nearly fell out of Scout's arms, so anxious was he to get down and get at that meat before Gert could eat it all.

"You don't blame us for what happened to your brother?" Geeta asked.

"No," Sparrow said around a mouthful of bread. "He knew it was risky, but he said he had to do it. And that was only partly for Seeta and the rest of you. Mostly it was because the Months needed him to do it. And he knew how important that was, even though he didn't exactly know who the Months were. It's kind of sad he never got to meet them. You can talk to them about him if you like. They valued him highly."

Emilie started to scoff, but quickly pretended she was coughing. She exchanged a glance with Scout, and Scout knew they were both thinking the same thing. The Months seemed to value everyone highly. But words were cheap. When it really mattered, what would they do to show what that value meant to them?

Scout was afraid that they would soon find out, and that Seeta was going to be their test case.

11

SCOUT HAD ONLY MADE it through half of the food that Sparrow had piled up on her plate before Caleb returned, hands still folded together as he indicated with his head they should follow him. He had to make the gesture; Scout wasn't sure what the bright green liquid everyone was drinking was, but the smugglers around them were talking louder and louder, their cheeks flushing even as they poured themselves a fourth or fifth measure of the stuff.

Geeta, having barely touched her food, leapt to her feet to follow Caleb. Emilie split one of the rolls and stuffed it with the rest of her meat before following after.

Scout caught the dogs' leashes to lead them out of the dining hall, but Shadow only took one limping step before sitting down with a soft whine.

Nothing was broken, but he was definitely hurt. Scout picked him up, putting out a knee to keep a jealous Gert from jumping up and nipping at his back legs.

"Do you want me to help with her?" Sparrow asked, her eyes shining.

"Can you?" Scout asked. "Are you familiar with dogs?"

"No," Sparrow admitted. "If I hold this end, she'll just come along?"

"If she wants to," Scout said, but, of course, as soon as she started walking out of the room, Gert rushed to follow, almost managing to rip the leash from Sparrow's hands. But the girl quickly recovered, falling into a trot beside the dog.

Caleb led them through a labyrinth of metallic tunnels, and Scout reminded herself that when she had the chance to ask all her questions, how they had fashioned this ship would definitely have to be one of them. Not that she thought she could understand the answer, but Emilie would be able to explain it to her.

The last corridor opened out onto a vast open space like the marketplace in the last station they had been in, except it was more than twice the size and full of life. Instead of displaying the uniformity of white building components, this marketplace had been designed by whatever this ragtag group of smugglers and black marketers had at hand, nearly as wide ranging as the goods they were selling. It far exceeded what the black market on *Amatheon Orbiter 1* had had on offer, not just in number but in variety.

Caleb kept looking back to be sure they were still following him. Perhaps nervous they would get swept up in the throng or distracted by something in one of the shops. Emilie nearly did, stuffing the last of her makeshift sandwich in her mouth to run her hands over a supple, glistening sheet of some strange plasticky material that displayed continually updating streams of data. Scout had no idea what the point of that could be, but it took a hard nudge to bring Emilie out of her reverie, and then they both had to jog to catch up.

Geeta didn't seem to notice any of it. Her eyes were only scanning directly in front of her, more focused on seeing any sign of the hospital even than being sure she didn't collide with other pedestrians or with the jutting counters of the stall-like shops.

Caleb ducked down a side street between a café serving baked goods and coffee and a smaller shop filled with brightly colored clothing. Then they were back in a narrow, featureless hallway. This one had a much lower ceiling than the ones around the audience chamber had, and the light reflecting off that closer ceiling filled the corridor with light almost too intensely.

"Sanitizers," Caleb said, although none of them had asked. "For the safety of the patients. Otherwise, of course, you wouldn't be able to bring dogs in here."

"My dog is hurt," Scout said.

Caleb looked back at her and Shadow in her arms. "I am sorry. Yes, of course, we'll tend to him as well. But let's see Seeta first, yes?"

He smiled at them each in turn and then continued down the bright hallway. He was walking more slowly here; perhaps the sanitization needed time to work.

Scout closed her eyes and tried to sense whatever was happening, but she didn't feel a thing, not so much as a tingle. Well, she would have to take his word for it that something was happening. Why would he lie?

At the end of the hallway was a small, round room completely dominated by a large, curving desk. No one was sitting behind that desk. To either side was a set of double doors that appeared to be made of some sort of opaque glass or plastic. Scout could see the shadows of people moving on the other side, but no sound carried through the material.

Caleb stepped up to the desk and tapped the surface. Then he pressed his palm to a glowing rectangle, and the door to the left lit up with a soft green.

"This way," he said. The doors opened of their own accord as he approached. He stepped to one side in the open doorway and let the three of them pass before jogging to the front to lead the way again.

Where the aesthetic of the main bulk of the ship had been one of tunneled solid metal, and the aesthetic of the marketplace had favored thrown-together bits of whatever was handy, here everything was that same warm, opaque glass that glowed from within softly. The colors clearly had meaning; the walls were all a uniform white with the slightest tinge of blue, but the doors were green, red, pink, indigo, and dozens of other colors.

Caleb seemed to know where he was going, walking briskly and occasionally looking back to make sure they were all still with him between trading nods of greeting with the few people they passed in the hallways.

The people all wore white leggings and tunics, but on their chests were badges that also seemed to be color-coded.

Caleb stepped up to another pair of double doors glowing green and once more triggered them to open, then waited for the others to go through ahead of him.

The first thing Scout heard was the faint hiss of air moving. It reminded her of her time in the medical pod back on *Amatheon Orbiter 1*, although that had been soft puffs of air across her face. This was more continuous.

She followed Geeta and Emilie into the room and saw a short, round woman with close-cut black hair and a face defined by well-worn smile lines.

Then Geeta gave a little cry and rushed past the woman to bend over what looked like a coffin fashioned from the same clear material as the rest of the hospital, only less opaque and not glowing. Seeta lay within. No—floated. Scout bent to look under Seeta's back but saw nothing between her body and the padded bottom of the pod. Scout had seen hover carts before, but those were magnetic. What held Seeta aloft in the air, blowing past her as if she were flying? She looked like something from a fairy tale, her hair fluttering around her face and rippling against her back all the way to her hips.

"Is she all right?" Scout asked, turning to look back at Caleb, then at Emilie. Did Emilie know how that floating effect worked?

"This is Dr. Tajaki," Caleb said to the three of them.

"No relation," Dr. Tajaki said with a soft smile.

"She is in charge of your sister's care and can answer all of your questions," Caleb said.

"But is she all right?" Scout repeated.

Geeta turned from the coffin to look at the doctor.

"We are doing our very best, but I don't want to make any false promises," Dr. Tajaki said. "Your sister has been through a life-ending trauma. She was put into cold stasis, and I'm sure with the technology you had at hand, that was absolutely the best choice. Certainly, it brought her to my care before deterioration set in."

"She's not cold anymore," Geeta said, pressing her hand to the side of the coffin.

"No, you are correct," Dr. Tajaki said with another little smile. "Cold stasis is prone to certain side effects in rare cases. Current protocols call for a warm stasis. This prevents the possibility of ice crystals forming in the major organs."

"Could that have happened already?" Geeta asked.

"The chance is very remote, but it does happen. We are transitioning her to a warm stasis, which is much safer. We are warming her very slowly, as that is the safest method."

"Will she wake up?" Geeta asked, looking down at her sister's face. She certainly seemed like she was only sleeping, now that she was no longer covered in a fine coating of frost.

"Oh no, my dear," Dr. Tajaki said. "She is still in a state between life and death. Even on this ship, we don't have the equipment necessary to attempt to revive her from stasis. But you will have access to that in Galactic Central, and I will oversee the procedure myself."

"It's not like a coma?" Emilie asked.

"No. Her heart rate and breathing are not just slowed down, they have stopped. But I promise we are taking the very best care of her."

"Thank you," Geeta said. Her voice was trembling ever so slightly.

"There are some things you need to understand. The warming will take several days to complete. Gradual warming gives us the best outcomes, statistically. That process cannot be interrupted. Of course, there is no reason it should be; I don't want to alarm you."

"I think we get you," Emilie said, trading a glance with Scout. Scout was thinking much the same: the doctor was telling them if they tried to leave, they'd have to leave Seeta behind.

"Could the entire pod-coffin thing be moved, say, to another ship?" Scout asked.

The doctor frowned. "I really wouldn't recommend that. Especially as there are no other ships in this part of the galaxy with a medical department capable of caring for her."

"But it's feasible?" Emilie pressed.

"I really wouldn't recommend it," the doctor said again, shooting Caleb a puzzled look.

"You are free to stay as long as you like," Caleb said to them, "and I will send someone from security to scan your palms so you will have access to this room anytime you like. If you should require anything, just speak aloud. The room will hear you. Now, Miss Scout," he said, turning to look at her. "Shall we see to your dog?"

Scout looked to the others. Geeta had pulled up a chair to sit by her sister's side and didn't look up at all.

"I'll stay with Geeta," Emilie said. "Do you want me to keep Gert with me?"

"Yes, thank you," Scout said. "I'll come back here when we're done."

She turned back to Caleb, who smiled at her and led the way back out to the corridor.

"Do you have vets here?" Scout asked.

"Our doctors are familiar with all forms of physiology. Any of them can help us. We'll just be going to an exam room a short way down the hall. I don't want to separate you from your friends too much."

Scout hugged Shadow tighter. "You've been with the Months for six years, you said? Has this ship been here the entire time? And no one knew?"

"A few were aware," Caleb said, opening a smaller door and guiding her inside. There was a low table set in the middle of a room lined with cabinets and an egg-shaped machine on legs in one corner. Scout set Shadow down on the table. He objected to the sudden loss of her body heat, but he was getting heavy.

"But doesn't it bother you?" she asked. "All of this technology and they aren't sharing it with the Space Farers. And no one is sharing anything with the Planet Dwellers."

"There are legal complications," Caleb said. "Believe me, I know your frustration. I work for the Months specifically because I want to see an end to all the barricades and embargos. And I think we're nearly there. But it's taken most of my lifetime."

He looked profoundly sad, but Scout still couldn't help asking, "Six years?"

"No, I've been trying to unite all of us on the surface and in space for a lot longer than that. When I was a young man, long before the war, I visited the surface once. I loved it: the land, the city life, the people." He lingered over that last word and seemed to drift off into thought, but then he took a breath and came back to the moment. "I did everything I could to return, but the increasing tensions and then the war made it impossible. Short of creating my own landing craft, which, believe it or not, I looked into, I was separated from what I loved best. But soon that will be over."

"I hope you're right," Scout said. "The technology should be shared, and the coronal mass ejection storms should be a thing of the past."

"Definitely," Caleb agreed. "Do you have people still on the surface, people who might be worried about you and your dogs? I have a way to send messages to the surface. Or at least I did; it's become unreliable of late. I'm not sure if anyone is still down there to hear me, but I'll be happy to give it another try."

"No, there's no one," Scout said, but something was bugging her. It took her a minute to work out that it was his eyes. They were so familiar. Then something inside her brain went supernova. "Who is your contact on the surface? What's her name?"

"Her name?" Caleb repeated. "It's Viola McNabb, but how did you know it was a woman?"

"Because you remind me of her," Scout said. Well, not personality-wise—in that sense, they were complete opposites—but there was no mistaking those eyes. Some of the facial structure was also the same, and the kinky gray hair. "You were her mother's secret admirer who lived in space. She kept every letter you ever sent her."

Tears sprang into Caleb's eyes. "Did she? She never answered. Not even once."

Scout stepped closer to the table and hugged Shadow close to her belly. She felt the sudden need for his warmth.

"I'm not sure when Viola's mother died," she told him. "She never said. I'm sorry to have to tell you, but Viola is dead, too."

"Viola," Caleb said, running a shaking hand over his mouth. "I did fear that. She never really talked to me, but she would pass things on, squawk her communications equipment, so I knew she was still there. But all of a sudden, even that stopped. Do you know what happened?"

Scout bit her lip. Viola had died spewing blood, poisoned by a trio of girl assassins who weren't even targeting her. She had just been collateral damage.

Scout hated that phrase.

"It was in the last coronal mass ejection storm," Scout said.

"That was a bad one," Caleb said. "Four days. I asked the Months to intervene when the Tajaki employees in space started dismantling those satellites, but they said their hands were tied." He sniffled, then turned to look over the counter behind him to find a tissue. He carefully kept his back to Scout, and she tried not to notice the shaking of his shoulders. "I had never met her—Viola. I had always longed to, and I was getting so close."

Scout tried to think of something to say, some words of comfort, but before she could summon any, the door opened with a soft hiss and a young man walked in, eyes on a tablet in his hands before lifting them to Scout and Shadow at the table.

"A dog," he said, his face lighting up. "I drew the lucky card today."

Shadow registered the man's growing enthusiasm and started wagging his tail, thumping against Scout's side. At least Shadow's injured leg was one thing that could be easily fixed.

The rest of her life and her mission to get to Galactic Central, what could be salvaged, were going to be much harder.

12

THE DOCTOR INJECTED Shadow with a single nanite and prescribed a day of low activity while the healing happened unseen inside of Shadow's body. Then he played with the dog for far longer than he had taken for diagnosis and treatment, gently tussling with him and rolling him over to scratch his belly.

Scout wondered if this was still going to be the norm in Galactic Central, that her dogs would charm the pants off of everyone they met. Why did no one in space ever have dogs?

The door chimed, and Caleb signaled for it to open. Sparrow was standing outside, Gert sitting close at her side.

"Emilie and Geeta are going to be staying in the intensive care wing, but I was wondering if you would like to walk the dogs around? I can give you a tour of the ship," she said.

"Shadow can walk short distances, but watch him closely," the doctor said, suddenly serious. "If he starts to limp or favor that leg, you should pick him up."

"Okay," Scout said. "Thank you."

"I think a tour is a splendid idea," Caleb said to Scout and Sparrow. "I myself need to get back to the Months. We are nearly at the barricade, and they will need my assistance negotiating the bureaucracy."

"Is it worse than Space Farer bureaucracy?" Scout asked. She had spent an entire day being processed there. Granted, she and her dogs had all needed medical care and food, but still.

"This is far worse," Caleb said, "because it's not routine. We're in the midst of a cutthroat legal battle. Scores of lawyers throwing everything they have at each other over even the simplest of actions. It's a miracle anything gets accomplished at all. But once we're past it, we'll be on our way."

"Have you been to Galactic Central?" Scout asked.

"No, not yet," Caleb said. Another wave of melancholy washed over him, and Scout could just imagine the dreams he'd had for the future that were all dashed now.

He was in pain enough just knowing Viola was gone. Scout was glad she hadn't told him the whole story. It would only have made things worse.

Caleb and the doctor stepped out of the room, but Sparrow and Scout lingered a moment as the two dogs greeted one another as if they had been separated for years and not just a matter of minutes. Gert sniffed at Shadow, especially at the site where the doctor had injected the nanite, but seemed to conclude that this was still her Shadow and not some Shadow doppelgänger.

"What would you like to see first?" Sparrow asked brightly as they turned and started back down the glowing hallway. Apparently, they were being sanitized again, to prevent hospital germs from spreading to the marketplace.

"I don't know," Scout said. "I don't even know what's on this ship."

"It's amazing," Sparrow said as they emerged into the noisy market-place. "It's not like on *Amatheon Orbiter 1*. No one is here just because they were born here. They *want* to be here."

Scout looked around. She didn't feel that vibe, but she didn't want to argue. Maybe she'd sense it later, after she spent more time here.

Or perhaps not. Sparrow had grown up in space, where life was very regimented. Scout had grown up inside the confines of a protective dome, but she had been about the same age as Sparrow when it had been destroyed. She cast her mind back to her first days alone with Shadow, crossing the prairie on her bike, finding little towns hiding amongst the tall grasses. She hadn't even known such places existed before her family died.

Those towns had been founded by people fed up with the rules inside the domed cities, preferring to find their own means of protection against the—at that time infrequent—solar storms. She had found their pioneer spirit contagious and had never spent more than a night or two under a dome since.

Maybe she did know what Sparrow was feeling. Freedom. But freedom at such a young age was scary and exhilarating all at once.

"Do you have a job here?" Scout asked.

"Not yet, but I will," Sparrow said. "The Months took me in because they said they owed it to my brother. They told me to just wander the ship until I found my place. So that's what I do. I watch people doing stuff, and if it looks interesting, I ask questions. Everyone is super willing to show you anything. I've learned so much more in the last few days than I ever did in school."

Scout smiled. She remembered that feeling, too. "What do you like best?" Scout asked.

A big grin spread across Sparrow's face. "Engineering. Do you want to see?"

"Yes, let's," Scout said. Partly she was humoring the kid, but more than that, engineering sounded like the sort of place that would have a lot of wide-open spaces and fewer people, particularly compared to the marketplace.

Sparrow led the way to the far end of the market, pausing only once to procure a paper cone filled with fried dough dusted with cinnamon and sugar. She shared this treasure with Scout. Scout had never had such a thing, but it didn't disappoint. How could something that was largely air on the inside be so delightful?

Then they were back in the part of the ship that looked like it had been tunneled from a single brick of metal. Each turn Sparrow took brought them to a hallway even more sparsely lit until they were so deep inside the ship the lights only came on as they walked under them and blinked out behind them. Scout had walked through hallways like that before on *Amatheon Orbiter 1*, but she still found the experience more than a little unsettling.

"You'll like my engineering friend," Sparrow said as they walked. "He's been to the surface a few times. That's where you're from, right?"

"Right," Scout agreed. "Is he from there?"

"No, just visits," Sparrow said.

"Like secret spy stuff?"

"Yeah, I think," Sparrow said. "He is one of the sneakier pilots. He can get down and back without the upper management at *Amatheon Orbiter 1* even knowing he's there. They watch pretty closely, you know."

"I got that impression," Scout said. "What does he do?"

"Uh, maybe he'd better explain that," Sparrow said, her cheeks flushing brightly enough to be apparent even with her dark skin in the dim lighting. "Sometimes I talk too much."

"Understood. I won't press you," Scout said.

"Here we are," Sparrow said, taking a few running steps forward into the cavernous space at the end of the corridor. Gert trotted at her side, giving a happy bark that was lost in the immensity of the space.

A few lights were spaced along the walls, hooded to direct their light down to the floor. But most of the light came from a glowing blue cylinder sitting in the middle of the room. It glowed too intensely to look directly at, and yet the room around it was so large that even this light could barely reach the walls and the ceiling high above was lost to shadow.

"This is the engine!" Sparrow said, running again with Gert keeping pace beside her. "It's what makes the ship so fast. It bends space-time!"

Scout had no clue what that could even mean. She nodded and smiled, picking up Shadow to carry him inside. It felt like her footsteps should be echoing in such a large, empty space, but something was swallowing up all the sounds, even Sparrow's voice, as she ran too far ahead of Scout. Scout walked faster until she reached where Sparrow stood at the very end of the glowing cylinder.

"What did you say?" Scout asked.

"I said, isn't it awesome?" Sparrow shouted. Scout would swear that glowing thing was sucking in all her words. Even standing next to her, Scout could barely catch them.

Scout looked up at the cylinder. It pulsated from white to blue, and

Scout had the disturbing sensation that it was looking at her, all the way inside her.

Judging her.

"Maybe you want to step back."

Scout took a moment to put the sounds together in her head to form words, then another moment to realize it wasn't Sparrow speaking that time. Then a hand closed on her shoulder, gently guiding her back.

That pulsating… it didn't seem to be making a sound, and yet something in her chest heard it. Not a feeling like when she was close to a rocket launching and felt that low rumble in her chest; this was different. It was like it was humming at two different frequencies, and her ears couldn't hear it, but her heart could.

"Keep stepping back," the man guiding her said, and Scout saw that he had put an arm around her shoulders to keep her moving, step after step, further back from that glowing thing.

"What is that?" Scout asked. Her voice sounded hoarse, like she hadn't used it in days.

"Just the engine," the man said. "Some people respond to it differently than others."

"Sorry, Scout," Sparrow said sheepishly. "I forgot about that part."

"Don't forget it again," the man said to Sparrow in a voice that was both stern and fond at the same time. "This was a mild reaction to the warping field."

"You didn't feel it?" Scout asked.

"Never do," the man said, letting go of Scout to continue walking alone through the semidarkness.

"Me neither," Sparrow said with beaming pride. "That's why I'd make such a good engineer."

"It takes more than that," the man shouted back. He must have learned how to pitch his voice inside this strange room. Scout could hear him quite clearly, even though Sparrow's words still seemed muffled.

"I have to study," Sparrow said.

"Was that your friend?" Scout asked. She hugged Shadow tighter and looked down at Gert. Whatever strangeness Scout had just experienced didn't seem to have affected the dogs at all.

"No, that's his dad," Sparrow said. "Hey, Mike! Where's Tom Tom?"

"Off duty," Mike said. He didn't shout, and yet it was like he was speaking right next to Scout's ear.

"I know what that means," Sparrow said with a roll of her eyes. "Back to the marketplace. Unless you wanted to see more here?"

"No, I'm good," Scout said, trying to swallow. Her mouth had gone almost painfully dry.

She had seen quite enough of engineering.

13

SPARROW AND GERT HALF WALKED, half ran back through the labyrinth of corridors to the now pleasantly soothing hum of voices that was the marketplace. Scout set Shadow back down to walk, but that meant keeping a slower pace. Sparrow didn't seem to mind. She liked promenading down the street with Gert beside her. The big black dog drew lots of attention and Sparrow soaked it all up like a sponge.

"He'll be in here," Sparrow said, ducking through a narrow doorway. Scout was afraid it would be another drinking establishment, like the one in the black market back on *Amatheon Orbiter 1*, the one she had been in when Sparrow's brother Hal had been murdered. But once her eyes adjusted to the dim light beyond the doorway, she realized it was something quite different.

The space was cluttered with squarish machines, some tall and some short, but each with a person sitting inside or two people sitting across from each other. Their hands were all moving at lightning speed, and everything inside the boxes was a wash of color and light, everything moving too fast for Scout to make sense of any of it.

And the noise! A cacophony of metallic clangs, grunts, screams, explosions, shots fired. But none of it sounded real, Scout realized. It was all a simulation. As Sparrow stepped up to a box containing two people sitting facing each other, Scout realized the clanging sounds were coming from the holographic forms floating between the two people: a man and a woman, both heavily muscled, fighting with great gusto with swords.

"Games?" Scout guessed.

"Yeah," Sparrow said. She sounded a bit embarrassed, like perhaps Scout wouldn't think such things were cool. It didn't seem to occur to her that this was something far beyond Scout's experience back on the prairie.

"Hey, Stewart!" Sparrow said to a man across the room focused on a single-player game. He looked up at her. "Where's Tom Tom?"

"In the back," Stewart said, jabbing a thumb back over his shoulder before returning his focus to the tabletop in front of him.

Scout followed Sparrow, matching her winding path through the narrow spaces between the games and up a flight of steps to a second, more claustrophobic space. Here the floor was packed, not just with the game boxes but with people standing around the tables, watching the players within vying against each other.

Scout was worried about the dogs, Gert in particular. Crowds of strangers made her edgy. But Sparrow sensed the dog's growing anxiety and stooped over to rub her ears and settle her down before pushing on through the crowd to a game box at the very back of the room.

"Tom Tom," Sparrow said to a boy about Scout's age. "I have a friend with me. She's from the Amatheon surface."

At first, Tom Tom didn't even seem to hear her, focused as he was on whatever game he was playing. But when he heard where Scout was from, he slapped a palm down the middle of the game board, freezing the play. Then he stood, extending a hand for Scout to shake. He was Space Farer pale, with dark blond hair shaved on the sides but long enough over his forehead that he had to flick his head to get it out of his eyes before he could look at Scout.

"I'm Tom Tom," he said. "You're Scout Shannon. I've heard about you."

"People keep saying that to me," Scout said. She had picked Shadow up when they had reached the crowded part of the room, and she shifted him in her arms now so she could shake Tom Tom's hand. "Are you that tight with the Months, then?"

"No, not really," Tom Tom said. "I do small jobs for them. They value my work. But I'm not in the inner circle."

There was that phrase again: *value my work*. "So, where did you hear about me?"

"Actually, it was down on the surface," Tom Tom said. "I have a friend down there. Technically, my contact when I make deliveries, but he's a friend, too."

"Tucker," Scout said. No matter where she went, she could never quite escape his sphere of influence.

"Yeah," Tom Tom said. "He told me all about you."

"I shiver to think what that could be," Scout said.

"All good," Tom Tom said, but there was a gleam in his eye, and the way he wouldn't quite meet her own eyes really made her wonder what Tucker had said.

"So, when were you last down there?" Scout asked. "Do you know how Joelle and Reggie are doing? Is Malcolm all right?"

"It's been a while," Tom Tom admitted. "Things have been getting hot, a lot more ships moving around in orbit than usual. I haven't had a clear path to get down without being seen. What would be wrong with Malcolm?"

"You're seriously asking me that?" Scout all but snapped.

"What?" He blinked at her, appearing genuinely confused.

"The Months have been nurturing his dependency on some drug," Scout said.

"I don't know anything about that," Tom Tom said, holding up his hands as if he were afraid Scout was about to hit him.

"You made deliveries to Tucker," Scout said. "Tucker was giving the drugs to Malcolm."

"That doesn't sound like Tucker," he started to say, but he flinched away from her and Scout forced herself to take a deep breath. Her eyes must be shooting daggers to make him react like that. Still, it wasn't like she could do anything with a dog in her arms. What stories *had* Tucker been telling him? "My deliveries were all intel. Current communication codes, other things we couldn't just broadcast down. No drugs, I swear."

Scout let the last of her anger go and gave him a tight nod.

Come to think of it, Tucker had gotten the drugs for Malcolm from Farlane McFarlane. It still ultimately led back to the Months, but apparently not through Tom Tom.

"Sorry if I got a little heated," Scout said. "I'm just worried about Joelle and the others."

"If you want, I can try to get a message down," Tom Tom said.

"To Tucker? No thanks," Scout said.

"Scout," Sparrow said, looking at a narrow band around her own wrist. It didn't look like the wrist comms Scout had seen before, just an ordinary red plastic bangle, but still, it seemed to be communicating something to Sparrow. "We have to get back to the audience chamber. The Months need you."

"I'm guessing there's no refusing a Months' request," Scout sighed. "Let's go then."

"Hope to see you again," Tom Tom said, and as much as his attention seemed to have returned fully to his game, he sounded sincere.

Sparrow and Scout got the dogs out of the crowd and back into the center of the street, and Scout set Shadow back down on the ground. Gert came over to nose him, her tail wagging like she really hoped he had noticed how very chill she had been in that crowd of strangers.

"There you are!"

Scout looked up to see Caleb coming their way, looking very grateful to have found them not terribly far from the hospital.

"We're on our way," Scout said. "Audience chamber, right?"

"Yes, that is correct," Caleb said, falling into step beside them.

"What's this all about, do you know?"

"There has been a wrinkle in the bureaucracy. Nothing disastrous, no worries, but your presence is specifically required."

"By the Months," Scout said.

"No, by the tribunal enforcers," Caleb corrected her. "Your consent is required on a small legal matter. But I will let the tribunal enforcers explain."

When they reached the massive double doors to the audience chamber, Caleb turned to Sparrow. "Thank you for showing our guest around, Miss Sparrow. Perhaps I can take the dog from here?"

Scout wasn't sure that was a good idea. Gert had never liked Viola, but then Viola had radiated hate towards Gert on account of Gert having caught Viola's cat, crushing its pelvis with her heavily muscled jaw. But Caleb held Gert no ill will, and Gert didn't seem to mind Caleb either, walking over to his side the moment the leash changed hands, tail wagging as she waited for this new person to pet her head. Caleb did so with careful deliberation.

"I'll see you," Sparrow said.

"I hope so," Scout said. Who knew what was about to happen? Her life kept taking drastic turns in the blink of an eye and Scout was all too aware that she could count on nothing, not even being in the same place for more than a heartbeat.

Caleb opened the doors, and Scout saw the Months on their dais, Mai seated and Jun once more pacing. At the end of the carpet were Geeta and Emilie. Geeta looked none too pleased to be there, scowling up at the dais out of the corner of her eye as she stood facing mostly away from them. Emilie gave Scout a little wave.

Scout raised a hand to return the gesture but didn't quite complete the motion. Her attention was caught by six figures who emerged from the back of the room and circled the base of the dais, three of them on each side. They stopped without quite meeting in the middle and looked up to the Months.

Tribunal enforcers, like she had seen when Liam had been taken away, with bald heads and long blue robes. Probably not exactly the same individuals, although it would have been very difficult for Scout to say one way or another about that. There was a variety of skin tones, but with the completely shaved heads and the body-hiding bulk of the robes, they were very hard to distinguish from one another. Scout wasn't even sure what gender any of them were, or if they even had a gender.

"Good to see you again, Scout Shannon," Mai said as Scout

approached. She stopped next to Geeta and Emilie, setting Shadow down on the ground. Emilie took Gert's leash from Caleb, and he gave the Months a bow before retreating from the room, closing the doors behind him.

"What's going on?" Scout whispered to the other two. Emilie shrugged. Geeta said nothing, but she fumed with anger.

"The tribunal enforcers called this meeting," Mai said. "There has been a wrinkle in our traversing the barricade, but once it's sorted out, we can continue on our way. Of course, we're all anxious to do that, right? Our court case and your sister's recovery both await our arrival in Galactic Central."

"Caleb said something about consent?" Scout prompted. That bit about Seeta's recovery felt too much like a veiled threat to her.

"Indeed," Mai said, smiling down on Scout. "The tribunal enforcers will be asking which side you are pledging with."

"Which side of what?" Scout asked, looking from Mai to Jun. Jun stopped pacing to lean against the back of her sister's chair. The two of them looked as unified as ever.

"Which side of the Tajaki trade dynasty," Mai said. "I understand your confusion. My sister and I are a little confused ourselves. We were quite certain we were the only members of the dynasty inside the barricade, but it turns out there is another."

She rested her chin on her hand and directed a sharp glare at the enforcers below her. If Scout had to guess, she would say the enforcers had been aware all along that both sides of the Tajaki dynasty had crossed the barricade.

"On what ground are we supposed to make this decision?" Emilie demanded.

"Exactly," Mai said, beaming at Emilie. "That's the wrinkle."

"And the solution?" Emilie asked.

"My sister and I are going to play host once more," Mai said. "My cousin of a sort is about to join us. You will be given an opportunity to get to know him, just as you still have the opportunity to get to know us. Only when you are ready will you announce your decision. I'm not sure how much you know about tribunal enforcers, but you should understand that there is no way for either Jun and I or our cousin to coerce you in any way. The choice is entirely yours."

Scout knew that wasn't exactly true, not with Seeta hostage inside the hospital, but she said nothing.

A soft chime sounded, and Jun rushed to take her seat before the double doors started to open.

"Emilie Tonnelier, Geeta Malini, Scout Shannon," Mai said as she rose to her feet. "Allow me to present my third cousin, Bo Tajaki."

14

THE MAN who swept into the room bore a strong family resemblance to the Tajaki sisters. He had the same brown eyes, facial features a bit more like Mai than Jun, the same long black hair hanging loose nearly to his knees. His clothing style was softer than the Months', nothing leather, all soft fabrics. His loose-fitting black leggings gathered a bit at the ankles, bunching up over his black slipper-like shoes. He wore an ivory-colored tunic with wide sleeves that extended past his knees, although it was slit at both sides up to his hips. As he walked closer, his own phalanx of six tribunal enforcers in formation behind him, Scout could see that the tunic, which had appeared plain from a distance, was actually intricately patterned with a thread the same color as the fabric, a subtle effect she found quite interesting.

His dark eyes glanced her way when he noticed her watching him, and Scout dropped her gaze, focusing on the dogs at her feet. She had a hold of both leashes just in case, but neither of them was having strong feelings about the man walking towards them.

The man was alone, save for the tribunal enforcers. There was no sign of the woman in black or anyone else wearing black clothes that fell just short of being a uniform.

"That's far enough, I should think," Mai said when Bo was as near to the three girls as the Months were. "You can speak from there."

"Indeed, I can," Bo said. He had a deep, warm voice that had the barest hint of a lilt, as if he were trying to be serious but was having trouble because he found everything so amusing.

"Just out of curiosity, how long have you been lurking in these parts?" Mai asked. Jun leaned forward in her chair, elbows on knees and hands to her chin, eagerly awaiting his answer.

"About as long as you," Bo said.

"And you think that is how long?"

"Don't play. We both know exactly how long it's been," Bo said.

Mai sat back in her chair and looked towards her sister, not so much to confer with her as to dismiss Bo from her attention. The smile was gone from her face, though, and Scout would bet anything that whether or not Bo was being honest about always knowing the whereabouts of the Months, the Months had known nothing of his.

Emilie dug her elbow into Scout's side and, once she had her attention, looked pointedly in the direction of the tribunal enforcers. Scout had been so engrossed by the dialogue between the Months and their cousin she hadn't been looking at the strange robed figures at all. But they were the ones actually in power here.

None of them had said a word, and yet now that Scout was looking at them, she realized they had been communicating with each other the entire time.

But it was a strange sort of communication. They never took their hands from where they kept them tucked inside their own sleeves, and they scarcely even turned to face each other. And yet, now that she was looking, she could see things passing over their faces: subtle little quirks to the lips and eyebrows, widening or narrowing of the eyes, flaring of the nostrils.

"Can they be talking?" Scout asked Emilie in a low whisper.

"They must be," Emilie said. "The real question is, can anyone else understand them?"

"I don't think so," Scout said after a moment's thought.

"The Months seem like the sort to play things close to the chest,"

Emilie said. "They aren't going to let you know all they know or all they are capable of."

"True," Scout said. "But if they could interpret what these people are saying to each other, I think they'd be watching them carefully, not talking over them."

Emilie looked up at Mai still looking towards Jun and Jun staring fixedly at Bo. Bo didn't seem to be looking at anything in particular. If anything, he was evaluating the room's decor. He wrinkled his nose, not finding some element of it to his taste.

"They know they're missing something," Emilie said, even more quietly than before, close to Scout's ear. Her eyes were still on the Months. "They don't like it. Any of them."

"Agreed," Scout said. Her cheeks felt hot, and she looked up to find Bo looking her over carefully. Scout fought the urge to try to smooth her chaotic hair down. He could wrinkle his nose at her, too, for all she cared.

But her cheeks still felt warm and tingly, and she looked up again. Bo was no longer looking at her, but one of the tribunal enforcers was. The other five behind Bo were actively communicating with each other, as well as with the tribunal enforcers across the room on the Months' side of the three girls, but this one just looked at Scout.

This one appeared younger than the others, although that was hard to define since they were all hairless with soft features. Their face remained still as a pond on a windless day, but there was something in their eyes. Scout felt like she was supposed to do something or say something, but she had no clue what.

"That one seems to like you," Emilie said, noticing the silent one herself.

"Yeah," Scout said. It was unsettling, being trapped under that intense regard.

Then, all at once, the tribunal enforcers all stopped "talking," dropping their eyes and bowing their heads, even the one who had been watching Scout.

"I guess they've sorted it then," Bo said dryly.

"Give it a minute," Mai said, her chin on her fist, still not looking at him.

The entrance chimed again, and another group of six people walked in, three men and three women. They were dressed in leggings and tunics like Bo's, if a bit less elegant. They all wore royal-blue tops and bottoms down to their shoes, and they walked with excessive speed in a squad formation.

Then there was a hiss of another door opening behind the dais, and six more people poured out to approach the sisters. These were the first people Scout had seen aboard the ship who weren't dressed like pirates, excepting Caleb. They wore long robes like the sisters, but the clothes beneath looked quite a bit more comfortable than the bodices the sisters wore.

Scout didn't know how it was possible to breathe in those.

The next few minutes were maddening for the three girls in the middle as each side huddled into a tight circle and whispered together while the tribunal enforcers studiously focused on the ground.

Scout didn't like feeling like her fate was being decided right there in front of her, without anyone conferring with her or even informing her of the details under discussion.

Emilie had dropped to one knee to scratch at the dogs' ears. Geeta just stood with her arms folded, the dark scowl never leaving her face.

"Permission to advance," said one of the men on Bo's side, his voice echoing through the hall.

"To the girls? Dream on," Mai said.

"I need to confer with my counterpart on your team," the lawyer said, unperturbed. "Where would you like me to do it?"

"Step over here," one of the sisters' lawyers said, waving for the man to follow her to the side of the room. The other lawyers watched them go, a few sharing whispering exchanges but most just waiting in silence.

The two lawyers leaned against the wall of the room and had a furious conversation, still all in whispers.

"Come on," Scout complained. Bo looked her way and gave her a small smile, just a quirk of one side of his mouth. It reminded her of Gertrude Bauer.

She didn't want him to remind her of Gertrude Bauer.

The hissing conversation between the two lawyers slowed down to a few parting shots, then the pair of them crossed the room to stand before the three girls.

"Just give us the shortest version," Emilie said the moment the first one opened their mouth.

"That's not optimal," the woman said.

"None of this is optimal," the man shot back. "Optimal would be a neutral third territory."

"No," the woman said.

"You're being needlessly belligerent," he snapped.

"Didn't you finish all this arguing before you walked over here?" Emilie asked.

"The two ships will be joined," the woman said, shooting a barbed look at the other lawyer to warn him against interrupting her. "Constant maintenance of the airlock between. You will be free to cross from one ship to the other any time you choose. This will be maintained for three days. At the end of the third day, you will have to announce your alliance."

"What does that mean?" Scout asked.

"The two sides of the Tajaki trade dynasty have been granted equal access to you," she said.

"Hardly equal since they came here first," the man grumbled, not remotely under his breath.

"You both violated the barricade," Emilie said. "How are you not facing sanctions for that?"

"All requisite fines have been paid," the woman said, and Emilie rolled her eyes.

"What does allegiance mean?" Scout asked.

"The two sides of the Tajaki trade dynasty have, for all intents and purposes, equal rights to this property," the woman said. "The planet, the moon, and all orbiting structures."

"It's our home," Scout said darkly. Emilie gave a fierce nod.

The woman summoned up a fake cheery smile. "Of course. That's why your input is so very valuable. The court will take into account which of the two sides of the family has the support of the employees of the colonization division. What you say in the courtroom could well determine who gains control of this property."

Scout bristled again at that word. The woman flashed the smile again.

"How are we supposed to choose that?" Emilie asked.

"You have three days to travel between the two ships and ask any and all questions you wish."

"And they have to answer?" Emilie asked, something like hunger in her eyes.

"Well, no. But a lack of answer is often answer enough, don't you think? By the end of the third day, you will choose whose ship you will remain on, and then we will all cross the barricade together and make our separate ways back to Galactic Central."

Scout felt like the woman was carefully holding back a lot of adjectives to describe the place she longed to leave behind—"the property"—and all she thought of it.

"And this is what the tribunal enforcers decided? When they were talking just now?" Scout asked.

The woman's smile wavered. "We do the best we can to understand their requests," she said diplomatically.

"You know they should be moved to a neutral territory," the man said again.

"Stop it," the woman snapped.

"What's neutral territory?" Emilie asked. "I mean, I know what it means, but where would it be in this case?"

"That's the trouble," the woman said. Her look of concern was no more convincing than her smile. "The only neutral ship in the area would be the tribunal vessel, and that won't do."

"Why not?" Scout asked.

"Their ships are… unnerving," the man said.

"*They* are unnerving," Emilie said, looking up at the group of tribunal enforcers still looking at the floor. "Do they never speak? I mean out loud? That would drive me mad."

"That wouldn't be the first thing to drive you mad," he said. The female lawyer rolled her eyes. Somehow, she managed to do it loudly. Or perhaps after observing the tribunal enforcers conversing, every gesture suddenly struck Scout as being loud.

"Many people travel on tribunal vessels without going insane," she said patronizingly.

"Explain," Emilie said, out of patience.

"The ships are invisible," the woman said.

"Made of a sort of crystal," the man corrected.

"Which is invisible," she said.

"Pellucid."

"I get it," Emilie said. "You're in a ship, but you can't see the floor or the walls or the ceiling."

"Nothing but stars," the woman said.

"With the added thrill of seeing everyone else in the ship with you and everything they are doing at every moment. And they can see you."

Scout and Emilie traded a glance and a shiver.

"So you can thank me for taking that off the table," the woman said brightly. "And just to be clear, I represent the Months."

"She didn't take it off the table out of kindness to you," the man said. "The Months had first access to you. They have an unfair advantage. I do hope you'll take that into account when conducting your interviews."

"Interviews," Emilie repeated. "This is starting to sound a lot like homework."

"They have Seeta," Scout said, and Geeta finally came out of whatever mental place she had sunk down to and looked up at the lawyers.

"We're working on that," the man said. "Their doctor insists it isn't safe to move her. Second opinions are going to be tough all the way out here, but we're trying to get one. Clearly, the doctor is biased."

"Because she's a Tajaki?" the woman scoffed. "She's as much related to your client as to mine."

"Which is to say not at all," the man agreed. "It's a common enough name. But she's a vested employee of your clients. That makes her partial."

"You accuse her of putting her employers' monetary interests ahead of her own patient's health?"

"Please," Emilie said, putting up both of her hands in surrender.

"Clearly, the two of you can argue all day. But we're anxious to get back to Seeta. May we go?"

"Of course," the woman said, and this time her smile came scarily close to being genuine. "I do believe that beds have been put in that room for your use. I hope we didn't assume too much, but it seemed like you would prefer to stay near her?"

"Yes, thank you," Emilie said after a glance at Geeta showed she had lapsed back to quiet brooding.

"I know you've had a very long day," Bo said, not taking a step closer to them but letting the acoustics of the hall carry his sonorous voice to them. "Rest, you've earned it. I will call on you in the morning."

He bowed to the three of them semi-formally, smirked at Mai watching from her chair, then turned and walked out of the room, his ménage of tribunal enforcers and lawyers falling in behind him.

15

SCOUT SLEPT VERY little that night. Shadow, who always liked to sleep as close to Scout's belly as possible, would not stop licking at the site where the doctor had injected the nanite. Every time Scout got him settled and just started to drift off herself, he would wake back up and get back at it. He was so persistent it started to annoy even Gert, who slept curled against the back of Scout's knees. She popped her head over Scout's thigh to make a protesting sound that Shadow just ignored.

Scout woke in the morning to the sound of someone opening the door and opened one eye to see an orderly pushing a hover cart into the room. On top of the cart were a couple of carafes with mugs lined up beside them and plates filled with fruit and pastries.

"Good morning," the orderly said when she saw Scout watching her.

Emilie sat up on her cot, scratching at the chaotic mess that was her bed head. "Smells good," Emilie said, sounding like she was still more than half asleep.

"This one is tea, and this is coffee," the orderly said, pointing to the carafes. "And I also have something for the dogs." She bent over to open a small cabinet on the side of the cart and take out two shiny bowls filled with meat and gravy.

The dogs immediately snapped awake, diving off the bed to get at the delicious-smelling food. Scout had to sit up in a hurry, pulling her arms out of the way before she got scratched up in the mad dash.

"I think you're all set," the orderly said. "Remember, if you need anything at all, just ask out loud. The room will hear you."

She smiled and exited the room.

"Nothing creepy about that," Emilie said, looking around the room as if she could see listening devices. The opaque walls that had darkened while they were sleeping were back up to full glow now that they were awake. Aside from the light from within, they were completely featureless.

"Geeta, how are you doing?" Scout asked.

Geeta looked up from her sister, her face drawn with weariness. She was still in the chair she had pulled close to the coffin the day before, the cot behind her neatly made. Scout doubted she had slept much, and what little she had slept she'd been slumped in that uncomfortable chair.

"There's food here. You should eat something."

"Maybe avoid the coffee though," Emilie said, getting up to join Scout at perusing the contents of the cart. She leaned close to whisper to Scout, "If she doesn't get some rest today, I'm going to talk to them about giving her something. She needs sleep."

Scout nodded. Geeta wouldn't do any of them any good pushing herself so hard, least of all her sister.

Scout had just settled down in a chair with a plate of toast and fruit, a cup of rich-smelling coffee in her hand, when the door chimed.

"Are we supposed to give permission or something?" she asked, looking up from the cup she had been about to sip from.

"The hospital employees come and go as they like. It must be someone else," Emilie said. She stuffed the last half of her croissant in her mouth, then, voice muffled by the food, said, "Come in."

The door slid open, and Bo Tajaki swept into the room. He was in all black that morning, although the black of his tunic had the same tracing of pattern in black thread as his ivory tunic had had the night before. He smiled at them each in turn, then looked down at the food-laden cart and did that little nose-wrinkle thing he did, like none of it was to his taste.

Then he saw the dogs licking the last of the gravy from their bowls and dropped to a low squat, holding out his hands for the dogs to smell before carefully petting them around their ears.

"You like dogs?" Scout asked. Her voice had an aggressive edge she hadn't quite meant, but he didn't seem to notice.

"I've known a few in my day," Bo said, moving from Shadow to Gert at her frantically pawing insistence. "I love all animals. These last six years in space, surrounded only by humans, have been a bit of a trial for me."

Emilie just choked back a snort, turning to help herself to another croissant as Bo looked up at her quizzically.

He had that same ageless look as the Tajaki sisters, but Scout would guess they were about the same age, somewhere in their early twenties. Scout wondered if being part of a trade dynasty came with extra responsibilities, making one look older than one's years, or if the opposite were true and money shielded them from the need to take on any responsibility at all.

"I've come to invite you to tour my ship if you like," Bo said. He stood back up despite the dogs' objections at the sudden loss of his attention, although he couldn't help smiling back down at them again.

"I'm not leaving my sister," Geeta said.

"At least eat something," Emilie said, pushing the plate she had already loaded up and brought to Geeta just a little bit closer.

"I completely understand," Bo said. "You do realize we can care for your sister on my ship just as well as she is being cared for here."

"If there's any risk at all, however small, I won't move her," Geeta said.

"I won't press you," Bo said. "I do hope you will talk with me, though. I only ask for a fair hearing."

"Fair hearing," Scout scoffed. "There is nothing you can say that will explain away the assassins you've got roaming the surface of Amatheon and up in space."

"Assassins?" Bo said. He sounded genuinely surprised, but Scout was having none of it.

"Assassins," she said again. "Twelve-year-old kids with body mods and an array of poisons."

"And a woman with even more mods and a penchant for poison darts," Geeta said with deep loathing.

"I honestly don't know what you are referring to," Bo said.

"They aren't here with the Months. They must work for you," Scout said.

"I assure you there are no assassins in my employ," he said. "If you would come over to my ship, you can search it from top to bottom to satisfy yourself on that score."

"Just jump right into your trap," Scout said.

"You know the tribunal enforcers will not allow any of you to be harmed," Bo said. "I would give you my word I know nothing of these assassins, but I don't think you would consider that compelling."

"You said you wanted a fair hearing, but I don't know what could possibly be fair about it," Emilie said. "We have no way of verifying the truth of what either you or the Months tell us. I hardly want to spend three days deciding which of you spins the prettier lies."

"I don't want you to make any decisions flawed by ignorance either," Bo said, walking back to the door. He poked his head out into the hall, where a cluster of shadows could just be discerned through the opaque walls. Then he came back inside with a small black box in his hands. It was shiny in the bright hospital lights, but otherwise quite featureless.

Like most of the marshal equipment on the belt Scout wore.

"Here," Bo said, placing it into Emilie's hands. It felt like a practiced gesture, as if he had done similar exchanges with dignitaries or heads of other dynasties or something. Like it was part of a show, but no one was there to see it save the three of them and two dogs.

"What's this?" Emilie asked, turning it over in her hands.

"Try it with your glasses," he suggested.

Emilie looked at him, then picked up the glasses she had left folded on the little shelf under her cot before going to bed the night before.

The moment she had them on, her face lit up in glee.

"What is it?" Scout asked.

"It's an access node," Bo said when Emilie failed to answer, too caught up in all that she was seeing and navigating through with little twitches of her hands over the box. "It gives her full access to all the Galactic Central archives in my ship's library. I thought I would have to explain to her how to work it, but I guess she's a quick learner."

"And self-learner," Emilie said, her eyes darting rapidly back and forth as she scanned. "This is far beyond what I could ever find on *Amatheon Orbiter 1*."

"It would be," Bo said mildly. "That ship left Galactic Central centuries ago. This connects to my library, which is current as of this morning and will be refreshed every morning. Not that I think you'll want to catch up on Galactic Central news, but you can if you wish. You also have access to the official versions of my family's history, every law book ever written—anything you could possibly need to verify anything I tell you."

Emilie lifted her glasses to give him her complete attention. "It's plausible you could doctor this to match whatever you say," she said.

"Indeed," Bo agreed. "I recommend asking the Months for access to their ship's libraries to compare. That also gives you access to anyone on the network in the entire galaxy, if you want to find a legal expert to advise you."

Emilie took a long moment to think that over. "We'll see what I can find," she said at last, dropping the glasses back over her eyes and getting back to her frantic search.

"She's shockingly easy to win over," Geeta said.

"Oh, I don't think she's won just yet," Bo said. "Three days is such a short time to cover so much territory. Really, I should fire my lawyers and get some better ones."

Scout suspected he was joking, he spoke so offhandedly. And yet wouldn't someone for whom such things were a matter of course speak the same way?

"I don't think I can offer you anything if you won't let me care for your sister," Bo said regretfully. "Can I send my own hospital chief here to evaluate your sister and Dr. Tajaki's claims?"

"You can," Geeta said. "I don't think it will change my answer."

"Still, you should have a second opinion."

"A second biased opinion," Geeta said.

Bo picked up the plate of food on the chair next to hers to sit down beside her. Then he held out the plate to her.

"If you're going to be your sister's advocate, you have to take care of yourself," he said. "That means adequate food and rest and at least one break a day to get away from this room." He moved the plate a little closer, and she gave in, taking a slice of some rich red fruit Scout had never seen before.

"Do you want some of this tea, Geeta?" Scout offered.

Geeta, still chewing, gave a weary nod.

"I'm not sure who came up with this meal plan," Bo said, looking over the plate of food. "You really should have some protein here."

Geeta held his eyes for a long moment, not even glancing at Scout when she handed her the steaming mug of tea. Then she took a wedge of toast off the plate and took a bite before saying, "Room, can you bring us some protein?"

"On the way," said a disembodied voice from above.

Bo gave Geeta a pleased smile. He continued to offer her bits of food until the orderly returned with a covered plate in her hands. She removed the dome and presented the plate to Geeta. There was an array of meats, from bacon to slices of turkey breast, but she reached for the bowl of lentils in the center of the plate. The orderly smiled and handed her a spoon.

"Any for you?" she asked, offering the same plate to Scout. Scout took a single slice of bacon and immediately had the full attention of her dogs focused back on herself. "I'll just leave it here in case you want more later," the orderly said, making room on the cart. She picked up the dogs' bowls and set them back inside the cart's cabinet, then set down a larger bowl filled with water, clucking her tongue as if chiding herself for forgetting it before.

Then the three of them were alone again with Bo.

Bo seemed engrossed in watching Geeta eat. "You look quite strong for your size," he said.

"I do okay," Geeta said between bites.

"You worked security back on colony ship *Tajaki 47*, didn't you? I'm sorry, I meant *Amatheon Orbiter 1*."

"Yes," Geeta said. "I was an ensign."

"Did you like that work?"

Geeta shrugged.

"You know, once this court case is settled, you will all be properly back in the fold of the Tajaki trading dynasty. You won't be out here all on your own anymore. Your job prospects won't be confined to what one space station orbiting a developmentally delayed planet can offer you. You'll have an entire galaxy full of possibilities open to you."

Geeta swallowed a mouthful of lentils and took a sip of tea. "That's true, no matter which side of your family wins this little battle."

"Well, yes and no," Bo said. "I want to develop this place, to see it reach the potential it's capable of with just a little support. You would be amazed at what I can accomplish in a single decade. Actually, you can see it for yourself if Emilie finds the details for you. I like improving people's lives. The more I can improve with a single action, the better."

"But the Months are, what, evil?" Geeta asked.

"I was going to say self-serving," Bo said. "Again, the news stories are all there in the library. When they acquire planetary rights, they like to strip the planet of everything of value as quickly as possible. It's devastating for environments. It's murder on the people."

"I'll have her check," Geeta said. "In both libraries."

"Do that," Bo said, then stood up and set the plate back on the chair. "I'll leave you now to care for your sister. Please be sure to get a little sleep. A short nap will do you wonders. And if you have trouble getting to sleep, just ask the room for help."

Geeta made a noncommittal sound that Bo seemed to take for agreement. He gave her a bow of farewell that she answered with a dismissive wave. He bowed again to Emilie, who noticed him not at all.

Scout watched him head towards the door without a glance at her and felt her cheeks burning. It was like that first call from the Months all over again, like she wasn't even there. Shouldn't she be as much a Tajaki employee in their eyes as Geeta and Emilie? Or did they consider her a mutineer like the Space Farers did just because she was from the surface?

But Bo paused in the doorway to look back at her. "Scout, won't you come with me?"

"To your ship?" Scout asked, feeling like he was trying to lure her into that assassin trap, despite his assurances to the contrary.

"No, just to walk your dogs around. The little fellow should get some gentle exercise to keep his healing on track, and the big one clearly needs to burn some energy off."

Scout looked down at the dogs. Gert was poking Shadow over and over, trying to instigate a play fight, but he was grumpily refusing to engage.

Then she looked up at Geeta, who gave her the slightest of nods. It was possible Bo was trying not so much to lure her away as to get one of them outside of the listening room. He might tell Scout something more than he could say out loud inside the hospital.

"I'll come," Scout agreed, getting to her feet and fetching both of the dogs' leashes from the little shelf under her cot.

She wondered what this man would offer her. She didn't even know what she could possibly want. He seemed to know Emilie and Geeta pretty well, but did he know her?

She was half afraid she would find he knew her better than she knew herself.

16

IT WASN'T HIS SHIP, but Bo seemed to know every centimeter of it, anyway. He led Scout down the length of the marketplace to where it ended in a wide staircase with shallow steps spaced so far apart it was almost not even a staircase. The dogs trotted along beside her, occasionally smelling the air. Then they started to pull at the leashes, trying to urge her on faster.

"Where are we going?" Scout asked as she fought to keep a firm hold on their leashes.

"The park," Bo said, sounding surprised. "Did no one show it to you?"

"No," Scout said. Her tour of the ship had been a pretty abbreviated affair, limited to the places Sparrow liked best.

"It's perfect for dogs," Bo said.

"I guess so," Scout said as the dogs whined, anxious to move up the seemingly endless staircase just a little faster.

"You can let them go. Nothing will befall them," he said.

"I'm more worried about what they might do," Scout said.

"They'll be fine," Bo promised. "Consider it my first demonstration that I'm worthy of trust."

Scout gave him a hard look but decided he was probably right. The dogs could look out for themselves, and if Gert ended up mauling another cat, it would be on his head.

She bent to untie the cords from the collars, Gert first because she was generally calmer about it, but even she was jumping again and again, anxious to be free. At last, the knot slipped off her collar, and she turned to charge up the stairs.

"Hey, wait for your brother!" Scout called after her. Shadow whined pitifully but sat at rigid attention until she had the cord untied and he could make his way more slowly after Gert.

"See, he knows how much he can handle," Bo said. "He'll be back up to speed by this evening, I'm sure."

Scout wrapped the cords up into tight coils and slipped them into one of the many pouches on her belt.

"That was Gertrude Bauer's belt, wasn't it?" Bo asked.

"Yes," Scout said with what she hoped was a tone that would encourage him to drop the matter, but she should have known better.

"I saw her cross the barricade," Bo admitted as they slowly continued their climb up the stairs. Scout could see a bright light at the top of the stairs that had the warm yellow feel of real sunlight. "That was a bit surprising, a galactic marshal breaking a barricade like that. I did a little research and learned why she was there. Tragic story."

"Tragic ending," Scout said.

"I would have preferred she got her man, to be honest," Bo said, "but at least her man was got. And good riddance."

"She shouldn't have died," Scout said. "Do you know the details about that?"

"Just that she was there with you in that bunker," Bo said. "I won't ask you to tell that story. Nothing that involves eight of you going in but only you coming out can be a fun tale to tell."

"No," Scout said. She tried looking up again, even shading her eyes with her hand, but all she saw was the dazzle of sunlight.

"The governor still doesn't know the fate of his daughter and her ward," Bo said. "What do you think, Scout? Should I tell him where to find her? Knowing that in finding her, he will surely discover she was planning to betray him?"

"She hadn't decided that yet," Scout said.

"She took a lot of steps in that direction," Bo said.

"Stop offering me decisions that affect other people's lives," Scout said. "I don't want that responsibility. You decide what's best, since you know so much already."

"Fair enough," Bo said, tuning out the growing anger in her voice. Then he inhaled, filling his lungs deeply. "Stars, I love that smell."

Scout gave him a puzzled look but then smelled the air herself. It had a rich green aroma. The closest she could compare it to was the prairie after the rains came, when everything started to bloom, but it was far beyond that.

And she could hear birds chirping. Hundreds of birds, all cheeping and whistling and singing at once.

Then they were on the top step, and Scout stepped through an arching gateway to a space easily as large as the engineering room below, but where that place had been eerie and dark, this was filled with sunlight. The entire ceiling was lost to it.

A path started at the top of the stairs, and past the archway machined out of the metal of the ship was a second archway, this one of living trees. The trunks bent inward ever so slightly, and their branches extended over the path, tangling together over Scout's head.

On Amatheon, the only trees Scout had seen were the stunted, wind-twisted varieties that clung to rock faces in the mountains. That and her brief glimpse the day before as Emilie flew them over the forested continent.

Shadow and Gert came charging down the path, delighted that she had joined them. Gert collided with Scout, her heavy paws knocking Scout back a step as the dog jumped up on her. Then something skittered in the undergrowth, and both dogs pursued it, tails wagging madly.

"See? The perfect place for dogs," Bo said.

"You were right," Scout said.

"I've often thought of getting a dog," Bo said. "Just a small one, one I can take with me on my travels."

"If your ship is anything like this one, I don't know why it'd have to be a small dog."

"My ship is somewhat smaller," Bo said. "But sometimes I travel in a little one-seater, just on my own. I would need a dog about the size of your little one if I wanted to take him with me in that."

"Shadow," Scout said. "And the big one is Gert."

"Gert," Bo said, raising an eyebrow.

"For Gertrude," Scout said.

"That's a fine way to honor her memory," Bo said.

Scout just shrugged. She really didn't want to talk with him about Gertrude.

"I have a menagerie back home in Galactic Central," Bo said. "I'd love to show it to you when we get there. Even if you arrive with the Months. I don't hold grudges."

"What's a menagerie?" Scout asked.

"A collection of animals," Bo said. If he had noticed the pinkening of her cheeks she had felt at having to ask, he gave no sign. "I collect animals from all over the galaxy, and I have a team of zoologists who set up their living spaces and supervise their diets. I like to keep my animals happy."

"What kind of animals?" Scout asked.

"I have five sections to my menagerie," he said, as they strolled out from under the trees to an open space covered in green grass. Some of the stalks were turning to seed on top, and an occasional flower danced among the blades, but this was a very different sort of grassland than the red-gold, monster stalks of grain she was used to back home. "The first is my aquatic world. Most of it is saltwater creatures, but I have a separate tank for freshwater creatures and even an artificial river."

"Must be big," Scout said, only half listening as she looked back down the path for her dogs. There was a rustle of ferny plants, and then they emerged. Thankfully, neither of them had a little animal in their mouth.

"Next is the polar area," Bo went on. "Some people think the cold environments don't harbor much life, but they couldn't be more wrong."

"Ah," Scout said. She wasn't sure what the correct response was. She knew nothing about the animals of other planets. She knew a little about the animals from Old Earth from her school days, but that was it.

"Then I have a tropical environment," he went on. "That's always the first place I visit after a long trip in space. I'm always so cold every minute when I'm traveling. The tropics are hot and humid. It's the perfect antidote to cold, dry ship air. And the animals are so diverse and colorful. Really, you must see them for yourself."

"It sounds lovely," Scout said. She was starting to mean it. She, too, had been cold every minute since she'd left the surface. Emilie and Seeta had given her warmer clothing, but it was like her very bones were cold.

Although the bright sunlight of the park felt lovely, it wasn't quite the same.

"The fourth area is a temperate forest. Rather like what we just walked through, but bigger, and mine is full of butterflies."

Scout smiled. She had seen pictures of butterflies before, but never the real thing.

"Some of them are tiny, smaller than the nail on your littlest toe, but others are immense." He held his hands up farther than shoulder width apart and smiled at her. "They're fascinating."

"I bet," Scout said, watching Shadow's head bob up out of the grass before disappearing again.

"But the fifth is my favorite. That section is like the steppes back on Old Earth. It's larger than the other four sections put together, but I need all that space for my herd."

"Herd?" Scout asked.

"Herd of horses," Bo said. "Have you ever seen a horse?"

Scout shook her head.

"They are magnificent. Nothing in this galaxy compares to the feeling of riding on the back of a horse across the grassy steppes."

Scout smiled but said nothing.

"I really do want you to see it," Bo insisted. "I would like to build something similar down on Amatheon, so all the people who live down there can get just a glimpse of the great diversity the rest of the galaxy has to offer. Don't you think they'd love it?"

"I suppose so," Scout allowed.

"You could help me plan it," Bo said. "You could help me with lots of things if you like. I value the input of the native population when-ever I undertake one of my improvement projects."

Scout didn't answer, but she may have flinched a bit when the word "value" had popped up again. But he kept glancing over at her as they walked, clearly waiting for her to respond. She had to say *something*.

"I don't know what I could contribute," Scout said. "You'd be better off working with the governor."

"I don't think so," Bo said, all the cheer gone from his voice. "The people on the surface who call themselves your government—" He broke off, heaved a sigh, and started again. "I can appreciate why the workers rebelled. I respect it, even. But that was generations ago, and the people who call themselves your leaders now are not acting in anyone's best interest but their own. No, the first step will definitely have to be moving them aside."

"I don't like politics," Scout said.

"Who does? But there's no better way to negotiate what's best for the most people. You do know what the alternative is?"

"No," Scout admitted.

Bo blinked as if he hadn't expected that answer. "The alternative is violence, Scout. The strong take as much as they can, and the weak fight each other for what's left. Politics is how we find better solutions. I admit it's not easy, and it's frustrating at times when it seems like giving up would be the best answer."

"I don't know much about it," Scout admitted. "You know my history, right? Everyone else here seems to know it. My hometown was destroyed when I was ten. I've been on my own, working every day just to keep eating. I haven't been to school since I was ten."

There was no way he couldn't notice her face turning red with shame; it felt like she was radiating heat, her cheeks burned so intensely.

"But you can read," Bo said.

"And do basic arithmetic," Scout said. "I haven't forgotten anything I learned; it's just that I stopped at that point."

"But Scout, there's no reason you can't start up again," Bo said. "I can give you the resources to do that, to catch up with other kids your age, even surpass them."

"That sounds like too big of a gift," Scout said, talking half a step back from him and looking around for her dogs. If he gave her such a thing, she knew she would be grateful forever. How could she not be?

But that feeling of gratitude would mean a feeling of being in his debt. And he knew that she would feel it. He had studied her, just as he had studied the others—even Gertrude, apparently.

He knew just how to get her.

"We should get back to the hospital," Scout said, whistling shrilly for her dogs.

"There's no hurry," Bo tried to insist.

"No, the others will be worrying," Scout said, although with Emilie lost in the library and Geeta focused on her sister, Scout rather doubted that was true.

"All right," Bo said. "I understand. But I will come again to see you all tomorrow."

He bowed and left her alone with her dogs.

And with far too many thoughts running through her head.

17

WHEN THE DOOR chime announced Bo's arrival the next morning, Scout slipped outside rather than let him in. The dogs ran out after her, anxious to go back to the park.

"Is everything all right?" Bo asked, trying to look into the room before Scout quite had the door closed.

"Geeta is sleeping," Scout explained once the door was shut.

"That's good," Bo said. "And Emilie?"

"Lost in your library," Scout said, "although I gather the Months sent her something similar."

"I thought they would," Bo said. "Shall we?"

Scout nodded, reaching for the cords in her belt pouch.

"Allow me?" Bo said, pulling a bundle out of his sleeve. "I had my manufacturing people craft some leads for you. They clip onto the collars; they'll be easier to undo when we get to the park."

"Thanks," Scout said, taking the bundle from him and unwrapping it. The leashes inside were like silk through her hands. "Is this going to be strong enough?"

"Assuredly," Bo said. "I can show you the equipment we use to fabricate it if you like, but it's back on my ship. Tell me, do you have spiders down on the surface?"

"A few," Scout said, clipping the leashes to each of the dogs. Gert twisted her head about, trying to get a good look at the pretty new thing attached to her.

"The design of these leads is based on the thinness but strength of a spider's webbing. It's far stronger than it looks. We generally use it in construction settings, but it works for small jobs too."

Scout just nodded, and the two of them headed back out of the hospital to the marketplace.

The Months hadn't been by to see any of them. Scout didn't know what to make of that. Were the sisters willing to bet anything that they would all choose to stay because Seeta had to?

Could Scout even say that was a foolish bet?

Bo kept up a stream of chitchat Scout didn't pay much attention to as they made their way up the long staircase. It was indeed easier to unclip the leashes than to untie the cords, and they took up hardly any space in her pouch.

It had been a thoughtful gift, certainly less terrifying than the offer of an education had been.

"I have something else for you," Bo said.

"I really don't need anything," Scout said.

"Gifts aren't about needs," Bo said. "Or maybe I should say: the best gifts are about needs you don't even know you have."

"That's exactly what I don't like about them," Scout said bluntly.

"Feel free to turn it down," Bo said, "but let me show it to you first. Why don't we go this way, down the other fork in the path? There's a little secluded alcove where we won't be disturbed. What I have to show you requires a little concentration."

Scout let him lead the way, only looking back from time to time to be sure the gamboling of the dogs was trending in the same direction.

The path went through a thicker patch of forest, the tree branches overhead denser and lower, some even low enough to catch at her hair.

Bo didn't seem to have the same problem, Scout noticed with annoyance the third time she had to stop to get a clump of hair free from a thorny branch. And he was taller, and his hair was longer. How did he manage it?

Then the trees parted, and the path turned, and Scout found herself suddenly on the banks of a little pool fed by a trickle of a waterfall. The tree branches, interlaced far overhead, gave the light a diffuse, green quality, and not the smallest sound from the marketplace below carried through all the forest behind them.

"Here," Bo said, finding a wide, flat rock where the two of them could sit. Then he took another bundle out of his sleeve and delicately unwrapped the silk binding.

"What is it?" Scout asked. It looked like a curved rib cage of soft, pliable plastic.

"It reads memories," Bo said, picking it up delicately and draping it over the top of his own head, the spine aligning with the straight part of his hair, the rib parts wrapping around his skull to touch his temples and behind his ears and against the base of his skull.

"That sounds creepy," Scout said.

"I know," Bo said. "That's why I wanted to demonstrate first. I need a moment of silence to focus."

Scout nodded and sat quietly, hands folded on her lap. Bo closed his eyes. A soft light within the plastic of the device started to pulsate, slowly at first, but then brighter and faster.

Then Bo opened his eyes and took the thing off his head.

"What did it do?" Scout asked, but he didn't answer. He just took another object from his sleeve, an egg-shaped piece of crystal, and touched the end of the thing's spine to the egg. The crystal egg pulsated and glowed for a moment, and then the lights faded out.

"Here," Bo said, placing the crystal egg in her hands. "Now, look into it."

Scout hesitated, but it seemed harmless enough. She raised it to her eye and peered into it.

She could see a series of low, rolling hills covered with grasses bending and swirling in a gusty wind. The sky over the hills was a deep, dark blue, like nothing she had ever seen.

Then, from behind a distant hill, a blur of brown motion appeared, quickly disappearing between that hill and the next. It appeared again, closer this time, then dropped away again. The third time, she could finally tell that it was a horse running towards her. A horse, just like they had on Old Earth.

Then it reached her, standing before her and tossing its head, making the rich brown of its mane dance and spin in the breeze. It looked at her with intelligent eyes and bent its head to nose at her. Scout was so startled she dropped the crystal egg.

But, of course, it couldn't really touch her. And yet it had seemed so real.

"You see?" Bo asked.

"That was your horse?" Scout asked.

"One of them," Bo said. "My favorite. I miss him terribly. But we'll be returning soon, and I can introduce him to you. Now it's your turn."

"My turn?" Scout repeated. "What am I supposed to remember?"

Bo, who had started to lift the thing to place it on her head, set it back down on his lap and gave her a look of profound sadness. "Scout. You lost your whole family. Not just your family, but your home. Every keepsake, every recording, every image. I thought you'd like to have something of them you could carry with you always."

Scout looked down at his crystal egg in her hands. "I don't really remember them," she said. "I try, but…" She couldn't go on. She wiped a drop of moisture that had fallen to mar the surface of the egg, but then there was another and another.

"Scout," Bo said, his voice infinitely gentle. "This will help. It can pull out things you don't even know you remember. I certainly didn't specifically recall every blade of grass on my steppe, and yet you saw it. Give it a try."

Scout wiped at her face, but then nodded. Bo put the device gently over her head. Scout waited for it to tingle or something, but it didn't feel like anything.

"All right," Bo said. "Close your eyes and pick your memory. The last time you saw them, or your happiest memory—whatever feels strongest to you. Ready?"

"Ready," Scout said, closing her eyes. She tried to summon the image from the last time she had seen her family: her brother pulling at her father's beard, her mother waving at her as she pedaled her bike away.

But the image wouldn't come. Instead, she saw herself the moment the asteroid had hit the city, the moment she and Shadow had been thrown from the bike and cut with a thousand tiny shards—all that remained of the dome that couldn't protect the city from such an attack.

She kept her head down and her eyes closed, trying to summon the other memory. She didn't even realize Bo had taken the device from her head until she heard him sigh softly and looked up to see him looking in another crystal egg.

"I messed it up," Scout said.

"No, no," Bo said, slipping the egg away in a pocket. "I said to find your strongest memory, and I'm afraid you did. But we can try again, if you're ready?"

"Yes," Scout said. "I can do it now."

"Very well." Bo draped the device over her head again, and Scout closed her eyes, willing that other memory away and focusing on the scent of bread. Her parents had been bakers. The smell of fresh bread always made her homesick. Always.

This time, when she opened her eyes, Bo was smiling. He handed the egg to her, and she held it in her hands, almost afraid to look.

But she was more afraid not to look. She lifted it up to her face and peered inside.

There was her family, standing in the sunlight under an indigo sky so deeply blue not even the dome overhead could dilute it. Her father's beard was as thick and curly as she remembered it, and her mother's hair was the deep honey-gold shade that was also Scout's natural hair color. Her baby brother in her father's arms was plumper than she remembered, with a thick patch of dark curls centered on the very back of his skull as if it were a hat he had pushed back so he could scratch the top of his head.

Scout gazed into the egg for what felt like an eternity, but she just couldn't get enough of the details. Her mother's eyes had been green? Had she ever noticed that? And her father had a scar across his forearm. Was that real?

Scout felt a dog's wet nose pressed to her knee and lowered the egg to see them both there, looking up at her.

"Thank you," Scout said, holding the egg tight in her hands.

"I want to do one more, if I may," Bo said.

"I don't know, this is already so much," Scout protested.

"Just one more," Bo promised, putting the device back on her head.

"But which memory?" Scout asked. Most of her other memories were not so good, things better left to be forgotten.

"This is a bit of an experiment, but it's something I've been honing for a while," Bo said. "I want you to think of everyone you knew as a kid. Your family, but also your neighbors and classmates and friends. Don't worry about holding on to any one memory, just let them all wash over you. Ready?"

Scout nodded, closing her eyes again.

At first, she didn't think she could do it. All of that stuff was so far back in the past, she didn't even remember what any of those people had looked like. She had barely remembered her own family.

But then images started coming to her. The woman who lived next to her parents' bakery who had kept bees in her yard and sold the honey as well as jam and would let Scout have little tastes. Just to be sure it was still good, the woman had said.

And her teacher at school. Scout didn't remember her name, but she remembered the way she had worn her hair in a bun on the back of her head. Scout had never understood why, since she always had to dig underneath to scratch at her head. Who piled their hair against the itchiest spot on their scalp? It made no sense.

Then there were the kids in her neighborhood who would gather after school. There was one boy in particular who was good at making up the most fun games they could all play.

Scout pressed her hands to her face, but there was no stopping the tears. "I can't do more," she said from behind her hands.

"I think we have enough," Bo said, taking the device off her head.

"What was the point of that?" Scout demanded, angrily swiping the tears from her face. "They're all dead and gone. What's the point in remembering them all now?"

"Because they knew you," Bo said, putting another egg in her hands.

"I don't think I want to see this," Scout said.

"Please," Bo said, folding her hands over the egg. "I would scarcely want to show you something that would make you turn against me, now would I?"

"I guess not," Scout said. She still didn't want to look.

Bo bent to pick up Shadow and hold him on his lap as he scratched at his ears. Clearly, he was willing to wait all day for Scout to work up the nerve to look into the final egg.

Scout bit her lip, then lifted the egg to her face.

She had expected to see some sort of collage of faces, all the forgotten friends and people who had cared for her once upon a time, but that wasn't what the egg contained.

It was mostly white space, as if the device hadn't known what background to fill in and so had left it blank. But in the center was a girl, a little girl of about ten. She was wearing a shirt far too big for her and a snap-brim bush hat that nearly dwarfed her head.

Then the girl swept the hat away, spinning on the toe of one foot, trying for as many turns as she could before having to put the other foot down. Her honey-blonde curls were caught up in little pigtails, tied low behind her ears so they wouldn't interfere with the hat that she always, always wore.

"Me," Scout said, her voice barely more than a whisper. "That's me."

"That's you," Bo said, "through the eyes of everyone who loved you. That's you still, if you can remember her."

Then he put Shadow in her lap, Shadow, who was the only thing she still had from those happier days. Scout buried her face in the soft fur of his neck and let the tears fall.

She had often thought of all she had lost that day when the asteroid fell, but until this very moment, she had never thought that one of those things had been herself. Herself as a happy little girl surrounded by love. Someone she could never be again.

Bo reached out to squeeze her hand, but didn't try to talk to her. He must have sensed there was nothing he could say. But holding her hand, his grip both strong and comforting, said enough.

18

SCOUT RETURNED to the hospital room to find Geeta awake and Emilie out of the world of the virtual library. They were standing close together speaking in whispers, and they looked up, startled, as Scout came into the room. Geeta looked relieved to see her and not a hospital worker. Emilie did too, for a flash, but then she scowled at Scout.

"He got to you," she accused.

"No," Scout said, turning away to herd both dogs into the room and close the door before unclipping their leashes.

"Yes, he did," Emilie said, walking closer to her to examine her face. Scout felt her cheeks flush, but met Emilie's eyes unflinchingly. "Yep. You've picked a side."

"I haven't," Scout insisted. "I did accept his invitation to see his ship, but that seems only fair."

"A-ha," Emilie said, crossing her arms. "How did he get you? Promise you your own moon, or just gaze at you with those gorgeously dark eyes of his?"

Scout faltered with her answer, momentarily distracted by Emilie's assessment of Bo's eyes. Were they attractive? She hadn't noticed. She wouldn't have thought Emilie would notice such a thing, either.

Then she gave herself a shake. "It wasn't like that. Believe me, I've had that done to me once, and I'm never falling for it again."

She spoke with a shade more passion than she had intended, but it made Emilie take a step back and hold up her hands in surrender.

"Okay," Emilie said. "But seriously, Scout. What's changed?"

Scout thought about keeping what she had a secret, but that seemed like a lousy way to treat the girls who had become her friends. She pulled her hand out of her pocket and held out the two crystal eggs.

"What are these?" Emilie asked.

"Look through them," Scout said. She hated the way her voice was already choking up, but she swallowed it down and kept her gaze steady on first Emilie and then Geeta as she stepped around her sister's coffin to take one of the eggs. They both peered into them for a long moment, then traded a glance as they traded eggs.

Finally, they lowered the eggs and placed them back onto Scout's palm. Scout saw Geeta clutch at the neckline of her jumpsuit and knew she was really touching the little data recorder she wore hanging from her neck, the one that contained every video and image she had of her own dead parents.

"Sorry," Emilie said.

"He hasn't won me over," Scout said, putting the eggs back in her pocket. "But I did agree to go over there. Perhaps we should all go. We can talk to his doctors, tour his medical facility. Pry into whatever we want to. We should know, whatever we choose, that we made as informed a choice as we could."

Geeta looked back at her sister. "I can't go. But you two should."

"Do we want to be split up like that?" Emilie asked.

"It will be safe," Geeta said, settling back into her customary chair. "The tribunal enforcers won't let anyone cheat."

"They won't let them outright break the law," Emilie said. "But everyone here is furiously cheating as much as they can get away with."

Geeta just shrugged, not arguing the point.

"All right, I'll go with Scout to see the other Tajaki ship," Emilie agreed. "But only because I don't think Scout should go alone. But what about the dogs?"

"Perhaps they should stay here," Geeta suggested. "Bo might try to take them from you under some pretext, turn them into hostages."

Scout bit her lip hard, looking down at the sleeping face of Seeta under the glass cover, the constant warm breeze the rest of them couldn't feel dancing through her hair. It was far too late to worry about hostages.

"Room, can you ask Sparrow to join us?" Emilie said.

"She's on her way," the disembodied voice replied.

"Do you really think it's the room itself that listens and talks?" Scout whispered to Emilie.

Emilie grinned back. "Obviously not. It's a person listening in and answering over a speaker too small to see. We have that kind of tech back home. Still, any opportunity to encourage them to underestimate us is an opportunity not to be missed."

The door chimed a moment later, and Emilie let Sparrow in. Sparrow smiled up at them all expectantly.

"Listen, Sparrow," Emilie said. "Scout and I are making a little trip over to the other ship. We won't stay long, but can you hang here with Geeta? Just in case the dogs need anything."

"Sure," Sparrow said. "You're going to the other ship?" There was no disguising the disappointment in her voice.

"Just to see," Scout said. "We'll be back in a bit."

"We want to be fair," Emilie said.

"Okay," Sparrow said, but she didn't sound convinced. Scout remembered what it was like, that first year after her family had gone. It felt like everywhere she went, people kept abandoning her all over again. They had just been going about their normal lives. None of it had actually been about Scout, but at ten it was hard to see that.

Scout gave Sparrow a hug, which caught the girl by surprise. "The dogs were just at the park, so they'll probably nap now. I hope we didn't pull you away from engineering?"

"No, I was just wandering the marketplace," Sparrow said. "I'll see you when you get back?"

"Of course," Scout said. Then she and Emilie were out the door.

Scout had no idea where the airlock between the two ships was located, but Emilie had been studying both ships' schematic—among a thousand other things—when she was accessing the libraries and knew just where to go.

"I'm worried about Geeta," Scout said, keeping her voice low, although she had no idea if anyone was still listening in. "Bo seems a much more honorable person than the Months, and I think we'd be safer there, as well as it being a better choice for all the descendants of the colony ship *Tajaki 47*, but I don't know how we can make her see that."

"She doesn't trust the Months," Emilie told her. "We were just talking about it when you came in. But she does trust Dr. Tajaki. Geeta has a little training and a lot of natural gift when it comes to reading people."

"So there's going to be no moving her?" Scout asked.

"Probably not," Emilie said. "But I'm going to examine every bit of the medical area to be sure they have everything Seeta might need and then persuade the doctors to go over to see Geeta. Their words won't sway her, but her read of them just might."

"I suppose that's the best we can do," Scout said. They had crossed the marketplace and were back in the labyrinth of corridors carved out of the metal. Emilie kept them to the large main hallway, walking with sure steps.

"I'm not sure we can trust either side here," Emilie said. "What Bo told us appears true, but there are lots of little things that aren't quite right. I think he skirts the laws a bit more adeptly than the Months. He hides what he's up to better. The Months didn't even know he was here, and they have access to the same tech he does. I think that makes him more dangerous."

"To us?" Scout asked.

"Maybe not the three of us," Emilie said. "But to all the people of Amatheon? He might not be the best choice."

"I wish the Torreses had got to us first," Scout said, dropping her voice even lower.

"We all wish that," Emilie said. "And yet they didn't. We have to go on from where we are."

The airlock meshed perfectly with the end of the hallway; the only sign they were in a different space was the walls going from machined metal to a bright white plasticky material.

Bo's ship was nothing like the Months' ship. When they reached the end of the airlock, the corridor became a rich, honey-gold material that Scout just had to touch. It felt warm, like a living thing.

"Wood?" Scout asked.

"A remarkable simulation," Emilie said. Her tone was trying for sarcastic, but there was no hiding the fact that she did find the material remarkable.

The lights spaced along the walls flickered warmly, like flames dancing over gas spigots, but that too was just illusion.

The corridor ended in a square room where two people were waiting for them, a short man of late middle age with squinty eyes and very pale skin and a woman of about thirty with a cheerful smile and her long, black hair pulled up into a high ponytail, the ends of it still reaching her waist behind her. Both of them were dressed all in royal blue, tight leggings over slipper-like shoes and long tunics. Frank had another sleeveless vest over his tunic. It fell past his knees, but Scout guessed what he wanted it for was the many bulging pockets.

"Greetings, Scout Shannon, Emilie Tonnelier," the woman said, upping the wattage of her smile a few ticks. "I am Rona, the first mate of this vessel, and this is Frank, the head librarian." Frank stepped up to Emilie with a little bow.

"Taking me straight to the library, I see," Emilie said.

"Not at all," Frank insisted. "Unless that is what you wish to see first. I am at your disposal. Name your destination, and I shall show it to you. Ask your question, and I shall do my very best to answer you."

"You're splitting us up?" Scout asked.

"Unless you object? Mr. Tajaki thought this would be more efficient," Rona said.

Scout noticed that only two people were waiting. Had they known Geeta wouldn't come, or just guessed?

"I don't see your dogs," Rona said, looking around Scout in case she had missed them.

"No, they stayed with Geeta," Scout said, but her eyes were on Emilie, silently asking, *Should we let them split us up?*

Emilie gave the smallest of nods before turning to Frank. "I would actually like to see the bridge first," she said.

"Certainly. Right this way," Frank said, making a sweeping gesture with his hands.

"And you?" Rona asked Scout.

"I'm not sure what I should see," Scout admitted. "Emilie is the one who knows how to evaluate stuff."

"I have a standard tour I give to visiting dignitaries. Shall we start with that?" Rona offered.

"Sure," Scout said.

"Feel free to interrupt me at any time. I'm here to serve you," Rona said. "Mr. Tajaki is dealing with a business matter at the moment, but he will signal me when he is ready to receive you."

"Okay," Scout said. She felt very out of place all of a sudden. It was probably the phrase "visiting dignitaries" that had done it.

Rona smiled again and gestured for Scout to accompany her down a different hallway than Frank had taken Emilie.

"The wood and gaslights are nice," Scout said as they walked side by side down the long corridor.

"Aren't they? It's one of my favorite looks as well. But Mr. Tajaki creates new decorative programs every so often, so the look of the ship changes at his whim. But they are all lovely," she was quick to add. "Mr. Tajaki has excellent taste."

"Do you have a park here like they do on the other ship?" Scout asked.

"Indeed, we do," Rona said. "A bit smaller, but then so is the ship." She paused to exchange nods with a couple passing the other way. They also wore all royal blue; the woman wore a long skirt and the man's arms were bare but he had a hood up over his head.

This variety of all-royal-blue outfits was making her nervous. It was eerily like the people in the black not-uniforms who had kidnapped and tortured Liam and later instigated the violence that had killed so many of Emilie and the Malini sisters' friends.

Not to mention the woman in black who had pushed Seeta out into space.

"Is something the matter?" Rona asked.

"Why all the blue?" Scout asked.

"Oh, that's just the current thing," Rona said with a dismissive wave. "Like the wood and lights, that changes when Mr. Tajaki grows tired of it."

"And everyone just goes along?" Scout asked.

"I don't understand," Rona said with a little frown.

"You don't get to pick what you wear?"

"Of course we do," Rona said. "Well, the tunic and leggings are required when I'm on duty, but when I'm off duty, I can wear what I like."

"But it will be all the same shade of blue," Scout said.

"When that's what Mr. Tajaki has chosen," Rona said. "All of our clothing is provided for us by the Tajaki trade dynasty. It's the very finest in the galaxy. You'll always be at a comfortable temperature. It adjusts to fit you even if you indulge a bit and your size changes, and it compensates for people with sensitivities to scratchy or rough fabrics. It's fantastic."

"But when he wants it to be blue, he programs it all to be blue," Scout said.

"He changes it up before we're all sick of it," Rona said. "I'm hoping for red next. I look stunning in red."

"But he wore ivory when I met him," Scout said. She cast her mind back to that very morning. She hadn't really paid attention to his clothing at the time, but she was noticing things now. "He's wearing gray today."

"But he's Mr. Tajaki. He's not an employee."

The corridor ended in a balcony, and Rona waved Scout to join her at the railing. They were looking down into a large open space filled with trees and grass and fountains. It looked like it was the heart of the ship, the arching ceiling above simulating sunlight streaming down through gleaming windows to light the little world below.

And everywhere were people dressed all in royal blue. Two women were wading in a little pond wearing skimpy outfits that seemed to be made entirely of strings, and even those strings were all blue.

"Isn't it lovely?" Rona said, tipping her face up towards the warmth of the artificial sunlight.

"Yeah," Scout said, because she had to say something.

The ship was beautiful, and the people inside it all seemed perfectly content, happy even. And yet the whole place was creeping Scout out.

Did Bo have something over all of these people? Blackmail? Hypnotic control? Or were they just this genuinely happy to have their whole world depend on the aesthetic whims of their boss?

19

RONA TOOK Scout around the entire ship, showing her the large cafeteria where the crew ate, the lounge at the prow where they could have drinks or snacks and look out at the stars, even her own snug little living quarters.

And it was all lovely, so much more pleasant than the bare metal the Months' favored or the rickety construction their black-market hangers-on preferred.

And the people were all friendly, greeting Rona and giving Scout a smile and a nod. She absolutely didn't fit in here, with her multicolored clothing and fading orange hair, and yet no one stared at her or even did a double take.

At least, none of the grown-ups did. And most of the people they encountered were grown-ups. But from time to time they passed a youngster, more often a girl than a boy, and never younger than ten or older than maybe fourteen.

And every last one of them looked Scout over like they were doing a threat assessment. And none of them smiled even when they greeted Rona.

"You have families here?" Scout asked.

"Something like that," Rona said with a smile that was less genuine than her others. Scout wanted to follow up with a hundred questions —where were the babies and toddlers, where were the kids her age, did they have a school here, were they also considered employees since they too dressed all in royal blue—but Rona suddenly stopped mere steps from the doorway to the ship's bridge and touched something behind her ear.

"Mr. Tajaki is ready for you," Rona said. "Did you want to finish the tour first? We only have the bridge left."

"No, I'm good," Scout said. She wasn't likely to see anything there that meant anything to her, and she suddenly longed to get this whole experience over with and get back to the chaotic colorfulness of the inhabitants of the Months' ship.

Rona led the way back down the corridor, away from the bridge and past her own quarters to a narrow, spiraling staircase. The lights were spaced farther apart here, casting some turns of the stairs in dramatic shadows. The stairs were so narrow that if someone below started to walk up, Rona and Scout would have to go back up to the last corridor to let them pass.

But clearly, it was a private staircase for Bo Tajaki's personal use only. And it didn't even need a door to close to make it off-limits to others. Scout was sure of it.

The staircase ended, and Scout found herself emerging from between two bookcases onto a balcony overlooking an immense library. Below she could see row after row of freestanding bookcases, disappearing into the depths of shadow long before they reached whatever wall stood on the other side.

The walls behind Scout were covered with bookcases as well, from the floor to the ceiling nearly five meters above, every shelf stuffed with books of all sizes, colors, and bindings.

"Is this real?" Scout asked.

"Quite," Rona said with a smile. "Books and artifacts both."

That word "artifacts" puzzled Scout at first, but then she noticed that between the bookcases behind her and the railing overlooking the library's main floor before her was a series of glass boxes on pedestals. Some were square, others low and rectangular, but all contained a variety of objects resting inside the cases.

Scout stepped up to the nearest and saw some sort of brass device. She had no idea what it did, but, given the number of arms and knobs and screws all over it, she was certain it must be complicated.

And the box it rested in had no lid. She could reach in and touch it if she wanted to.

"Mr. Tajaki's office is this way," Rona said, sweeping a hand towards the left side of the balcony, where a narrow staircase that appeared to be made of delicately shaped brass descended to the main floor. There was another like it on the right side, both making a slow progression of long, shallow steps that seemed to encourage anyone walking down them to stop and examine each of the shelves on the way.

Scout looked at the spines of the books as she followed Rona down to the main level. Some she could read easily enough, some had a sprinkling of unfamiliar words, but most were quite beyond her. She could sound out letters that made words she had never heard.

And still, others were written in sigils or swoops or sticklike characters that bore no resemblance to the letters she had learned in school as a child.

Scout was so caught up in trying to decipher those strange letters that she stopped walking altogether, realizing only after Rona had disappeared from sight that she had lost her guide.

She ran to the bottom of the stairs and pulled up short. But then she should scarcely be surprised to find Emilie in this place. The decorative touches of soft light and warm wood tones were nothing like anything she would ever associate with loud-and-proud Emilie, but whatever the trappings, the room contained troves of data. And Emilie was always where the data was.

"Hey," Scout said. Emilie had been scanning row after row of books along the shelf that ran just under the balcony. She looked up at Scout and seemed to take a second to recognize her.

"Hey," she said back.

"Find anything useful?" Scout asked.

"Too much," Emilie said as if it pained her.

"There you are," Rona said, her long ponytail swinging as she jogged back to find her lost charge. "Mr. Tajaki awaits."

"Okay. You coming?" Scout asked Emilie.

"No, but come get me before you go," Emilie said.

Rona smiled again, then led the way down the center of the library, glancing back from time to time to make sure Scout was still with her. The aisle they followed cut down the middle of each row of shelves and Scout looked back and forth, trying to see down each end of each row, to drink it all in. But it was all too much.

Had Bo read them all? Or Frank? Could anyone's mind contain all these words and charts and pictures and numbers? All this data?

When she reached the very last row of books, Rona drew to a halt so suddenly Scout had to stumble back to keep from colliding with her.

"Mr. Tajaki?" Rona said softly.

Scout rose up on tiptoe to see over Rona's shoulder. Bo was alone behind an immense desk, a desk of wood polished so brightly it seemed to contain its own light. Bo looked up from a tablet in his hands and looked impassively at Rona. Then he noticed Scout behind her and summoned a smile of welcome, tucking the tablet away in a drawer as he rose to extend a hand to her.

Rona stepped to one side to let Scout pass, and Scout came forward to take Bo's hand. Rona bowed and left without a word.

"Tell me, Scout, how do you find my library?"

Scout didn't answer right away. At first, she found it odd that he didn't ask instead how she found his ship. Did he think she wasn't capable of assessing the quality of a ship?

But then again, she wasn't. So why should he pretend otherwise?

And yet, she wasn't qualified to say anything intelligent about a library either.

"Come, Scout," he said, gesturing for her to sit across from him as he smoothed the back of his tunic before taking his own seat. "Are we not friends? Don't you know by now that I'm not here to judge you? I know what opportunities life has denied you, but six years is not so great a time as all that. It can be made up. And for someone as clever as you, it won't take even half the time."

Scout wasn't quite sure what he was saying to her. "Are you talking about sending me back to school?"

"Not exactly," he said. "There are other ways." He bent to open the bottom drawer of his desk, but paused to look over at her. "May I be permitted one last gift? I know how you feel about them."

"What is it?" Scout asked.

"It is a mere trifle by Galactic Central standards, but I think you will get far more out of it than the average Galactic Central teen."

Scout chewed her lip. He hadn't exactly answered her question.

"You can certainly refuse to even see it. I won't be offended. Or if, after you see it, you don't want it or think you shouldn't take it from me, I'll understand. I admit I'm offering it to you for selfish reasons."

"To make me pick your side," Scout said.

"I've never wanted to coerce you into a choice at all," Bo said. She searched his tone for signs of pretend offense, but he was speaking to her quite plainly. "My only hope is that you will see who I am and who my people are and judge us by our merits. My gift is selfish, I admit, because I think with it you will be better able to judge the truth of things."

Scout all but squirmed in her seat. Clearly, he wasn't just going to tell her what he had. She didn't trust her voice to speak, so she just gave a nod, a very quick one lest she change her mind before she had seen what he had.

Bo reached back down into the drawer and then set a little box on the desk in front of her. It looked like the access box he had given Emilie, shiny black but otherwise featureless. But this was smaller, no larger than the palm of her hand.

"What does it do?" Scout asked.

"You have a lens, correct?" Bo asked.

"One," Scout said.

"Put it on, then say, 'Hello, Teacher.'"

Scout pulled out the single, scratched lens she had taken from Gertrude Bauer. The other lens had been smashed when the marshal had fallen fatally wounded to the ground, but one had been enough for Scout to access Gertrude's tools.

Scout set the lens over her eye and felt that familiar suction as it adhered to her face. The lens compensated for the low light of the room around her, showing everything in far finer detail than her own eyes could see. In the corner it told her the ambient temperature and what looked like coordinates for where she was in space.

"Hello, Teacher," Scout said.

"Hello, student," said a voice. She couldn't tell if the voice was male or female, young or old. It seemed to be everything at once. Then she saw a faint outline, a human shape without features like a gray cloud, leaning back against the edge of the desk. "How shall I call you?"

"Um, Scout," Scout said, assuming that was what the gray thing was asking her. This was several degrees stranger than the computer on Liam's ship.

"Pleased to meet you, Scout," the form said, its voice still wavering between a thousand different tones. "I am a LaSalle Corporation evolving AI, educator class."

"Okay," Scout said, looking past the gray figure to Bo watching from his chair beyond.

"I am here to service all your educational needs," the form went on. "Do you wish to give me a name?"

"Not just yet," Scout said, then took the lens from her eye to look at Bo without the gray shape between them. "What is this?"

"It was my personal tutor from the age of ten until I finished my academic career," Bo said. "I reset the profile. It will assume an appearance based on your preferences as you interact with it. Giving it a name is the largest step."

"But what does it do?" Scout asked.

"Spend some time with it every day," Bo said. "It will assess what you know, where you lack knowledge, and the best approach to start moving you forward. It will find what interests you and help you pursue those interests. It will learn by what methods you learn the best and the fastest. With this AI, you will surpass other students your age within a year, I guarantee it."

"But I make my decision tomorrow night," Scout said.

"My gift is not conditional. The AI is yours, whatever you choose," Bo told her. "I do hope you will confer with your teacher. It can give you the rudiments of the laws involved in the case, the history, whatever you feel you need to know to make your decision."

Scout didn't say out loud, "If I can trust it."

"You'll be as informed as your friend Emilie if you wish to be," Bo added. Scout didn't like how it sounded like he was trying to pit her against her friends, and yet his tone held no mischief or malice. She was just being paranoid. Besides, surely he wanted to get all three of them on his side, not just Scout.

"Thank you," Scout said, taking the little box from the desk and putting it in her belt pouch.

"You will use it?" Bo asked.

"Yes," Scout said. "Yes, I will."

"Excellent," Bo said with a satisfied smile. "I'm afraid I have some other matters that need dealing with. That's the trouble with running a galaxy-spanning business."

"Of course," Scout said, backing away.

"And I won't be able to call on you tomorrow. Give my regret to your dogs. But I shall see you tomorrow night at the assembly."

"Yes," Scout said, not sure what else she could say.

Bo took the tablet out of its drawer and set it on top of his desk, scanning and reading, frowning and jabbing at the screen, then reading some more. If he noticed Scout still lingering in the shadows of the last row of bookcases, he said nothing.

And even alone, he revealed nothing. Scout wanted to believe he was honest.

But she wasn't sure she could.

20

SCOUT SLEPT LITTLE THAT NIGHT. She gave up at what she assumed would be about dawn back home and slipped out of bed, gathering up her shoes and managing to sneak herself and the dogs out the door without waking the others.

A hospital worker sitting in a chair just down the hall from the room looked up as she stepped out of the room, but if he was there to guard them, he made no move to stop her as she clipped the leashes on the dogs' collars, pulled on her shoes, and headed out of the hospital.

The marketplace was as lively as ever, black marketers in their wide array of clothing spilling in and out of the various shops, gaming halls, and drinking establishments. None of them bothered Scout or her dogs. Quite the contrary; the persistence of their behavior, the basic honesty of what they wanted out of life and how they went about getting it, was refreshing.

But she left it behind her as she climbed the long stair to the park. They darkened the park at night to let the nocturnal animals that dwelled there go about their own business, but it was brightly lit again by the time she reached it. She unhooked the dogs and let them run.

She had decided just to let her feet take her where they wanted to go, but when she at last lifted her head, she saw to her annoyance that they had brought her back to the secluded waterfall.

Although perhaps that made sense. She sat down on the flat rock, took out the little AI box, and set it on the rock before her.

She didn't know why she hadn't told Geeta or Emilie about it. She had decided she wasn't going to lie or hide things from them, and then she had without even thinking.

She could go back now, wake them up, show them what she had. Maybe Emilie could look at it, see if it was a trick or not. That would be the sensible thing to do.

Instead, she took the lens out of her pocket and placed it over her eye. "Hello, Teacher," Scout said.

"Hello, Scout," the gray form said. It was sitting on the rock before her, mirroring her own cross-legged posture, the little box between them. "Have you chosen a name for me yet?" the AI asked.

"No," Scout said. "I will."

"Where would you like to begin?" the AI asked.

"What do you already know? Not, like, galactic knowledge," she quickly amended. "What do you know about me and what I'm doing here?"

"Since you accepted me from my former student, I have scanned all available networks for information about you, including the information stored on the tablet in your belt," the AI told her.

"So basically you know everything," Scout said.

"Basically," the AI agreed.

"So, if you were me, in this situation now, what would you do?" Scout asked. Then she held her breath, waiting for it to tell her to choose Bo. Then she could just shut it off and bring it to Emilie.

"Don't you know what you want to do?" the AI asked.

"I don't know what I should do," Scout said.

"But what do you *want* to do?" the AI persisted.

Scout thought that over. She had seen everything she could possibly wish of both ships. She had talked to Bo and listened to his explanations.

But she hadn't talked to the Months.

"You have questions," the AI said.

"Questions only they can answer," Scout agreed. "But what if they won't?"

"They certainly won't if you never ask," the AI said, logically enough.

Scout nodded, took off the lens, and put it and the little box away. Then she whistled for the dogs, reattached their leashes, and led them back to the audience chamber.

She was not surprised to find the sisters there, alone, waiting for her. Everyone seemed to know where she was, where she was going, and what she was doing every moment of the day.

"You wanted to see us?" Mai said, her voice a warm coo. Jun was also seated, not pacing this time, but scowling fiercely.

And she was supposed to be the one who liked Scout.

"Why are you running a black market in the Space Farer stations? Why run around the upper management when they're supposed to be working for you?" Scout asked.

"They are supposed to be working for the Tajaki trade dynasty, but as you know, there is a bit of a disagreement about just who they would be reporting to. The black markets let us get a feel for the people we hope to liberate, what their wants and needs are. Who they are as a people. It also lets us provide for the wants and needs their current upper management are not in a position to provide for," Mai said.

"And it makes you rich," Scout guessed.

"What we make from this particular facet of our trade empire is largely eaten up in legal fees, I'm afraid," Mai said.

"That's not her real question," Jun said. Scout flinched at the raw quality of her voice. She sounded like she had spent a lifetime screaming at the top of her lungs and now she was forced to try to form words from the thready remains of her vocal cords.

"I know, dear," Mai said, patting her sister on the hand. "But she'll get to it in her own time, don't you think?"

Jun just scowled.

Scout took a deep breath, squeezing the leashes in her hand as if they could lend her strength. "You have been stirring up animosity between the Planet Dwellers and the Space Farers," she said at last. "Your actions will bring about a war."

"You were already at war when we arrived," Mai said mildly. "We arranged your cease-fire, actually. It's a great shame we couldn't arrive sooner. Just a matter of days and we could have saved your town. So many resources lost, human and otherwise. Wars are bad for business."

"You are trying to infiltrate the rebellion," Scout went on.

"The safest way to dismantle it is from within," Mai said. "They have access to some nasty things and are liable to retaliate swiftly against any outside attack."

"You used drugs to manipulate a grieving man," Scout said.

"We provided him with clean, safe pharmaceuticals in lieu of what he had been taking," Mai said. "I know that was mishandled. Some of our underlings thought it would be good for their careers if they took some initiative in that matter. But they pushed too hard, broke an important connection we had been nurturing for quite some time. It was a grave disappointment for us. I assure you, the parties involved have been terminated."

Scout didn't ask if they meant fired or killed. She knew they wanted her to.

"Any other questions?" Mai asked, too sweetly.

Scout tried hard to think, but her head was already aching. In the fairy tales she remembered from childhood, there had always been ways for clever adventurers to trick others into revealing the truth, but those ways always seemed to rely on a logical solution. It would be easier to divide truth from untruth if they were distinct things. This person was a constant truth-teller, that person always told lies.

But everyone she encountered seemed to be doing both at once, almost arbitrarily. And she wasn't clever enough to sort it out.

"Go and take a walk if you like," Mai said. "Think it over. Consult your friends. Consult the professor you have in your pocket. Consult our dear cousin Bo. If you have more questions, we'll still be here. Just come back and ask."

Scout nodded and led her dogs away. Gert's back was a bristling ridge of raised hackles and she had been growling a low warning at

Jun since Jun had spoken. Shadow didn't like her any better. They should go before Jun got really annoyed and upset her dogs.

The sisters knew about the AI. They knew everything. Scout doubted she could feel more exposed, more on display for all to see, if she were on board the crystal ship of the tribunal enforcers.

Scout and the dogs wandered the ship for the better part of the day before finally returning to the hospital room. Geeta was napping upright in her chair, but opened her eyes as Scout entered. She nudged Emilie sitting next to her, who dismissed her virtual world to give the real one her attention.

"You've been avoiding us?" Emilie said. It was something between a statement and a question.

"Bo gave me this," Scout said, setting the little black box on the cart of half-eaten lunch food. Emilie picked it up, turned it over in her fingers. "Hello, Teacher," Scout said. Emilie glanced up at Scout, then jerked back as if startled by something between them.

But then she was still wearing her glasses.

"Evolving AI," Emilie said, handing the box back to Scout. "It's already imprinted on you. Or so it told me."

"He really wants you on his side," Geeta said. "Is that how you're going to declare?"

"I really think we should all be together on this," Emilie said. "They are going to split the ships after this assembly tonight. Do we really want to be on separate ships?"

Scout stared glumly at the floor.

"It's not so dire as all that," Geeta said. "We're all heading to Galactic Central. It's not like they're going to own us."

"They already think they own us," Scout said. "They're just fighting about which member of the family owns us."

"Once we get to the court and Seeta is safe, we can say whatever we like. They can't force us to say anything," Geeta said. "And surely the Torreses will be there. There won't be any barricade keeping them out."

"I don't think they have the power to help us," Scout said. "I don't think they ever did."

"So if it doesn't matter what we choose, the least we can do is choose to stay together, right?" Emilie said.

"The risk of moving Seeta is slight, correct?" Scout asked.

"More than the risk of not moving her," Geeta quickly said.

"But slight," Emilie agreed.

"And Bo will share everything with us. We can spend every day in his library researching everything. By the time we got to Galactic Central, we'd know what our rights are."

"The Months have a library too," Geeta said.

"Which they didn't offer us until we already had Bo's," Scout said. "What will change as soon as that airlock detaches? Do we go back to having access to nothing?"

"That could be true no matter what side we end up on," Geeta said.

"I just feel like the Months want Amatheon only for what wealth they can extract from it. Because they've been extracting it already through their black markets. But Bo says he wants to make life better, to bring in the technology to make Amatheon like any planet in Galactic Central."

"He says," Emilie said.

"You believe him," Geeta said.

"I don't know," Scout said. "There's something weird about all the people on his ship."

"All wearing royal blue, you mean?" Emilie said. "Like the shadowy folks back home with their black outfits. It would make sense if he was behind the force working against the Months' people. More sense than any other explanation, even though he denied it."

"I know," Scout said. She had never felt more incapable of dealing with the world than she did in that moment.

And then the chime sounded, not the door chime but a larger, more resonant sound that filled every room and hallway of the hospital, perhaps the entire ship.

They all looked up towards the ceiling. The room didn't speak to them, but they all knew their time had come.

This time it was the door that chimed, and Scout opened the door to let Caleb enter.

"The delegates from the other branch of the Tajaki trade dynasty are here, as well as both ménages of tribunal enforcers," he said. "They all await you in the audience chamber."

Geeta pressed her hand to the top of her sister's coffin, then took Emilie's arm to walk out of the room. Scout gathered up her dogs' leashes and followed behind with Caleb.

For someone about to decide the fate of millions, she felt a lot more like she was walking to her own execution.

21

VOICES ECHOED through the audience chamber so loudly they could be heard even before the double doors opened. Caleb gave Scout's arm a reassuring squeeze and then moved across the room to join the Months on their dais.

Their lawyers and Bo's lawyers were once again in a huddle off to the side of the strip of carpet, arguing furiously. The six tribunal enforcers arrayed before the dais were once more standing with heads bowed and hands tucked inside sleeves, waiting quietly for the moment when they'd be needed.

Bo was near the door with his own ménage of tribunal enforcers and fell into step beside Scout as she followed Geeta and Emilie to the end of the carpet.

"Did you notice?" he asked.

Scout looked up at him, but he looked the same as before. He was wearing the ivory tunic again. She wondered if it had some special meaning for him, that he always wore it when confronting his scarlet-favoring cousins.

Then she noticed his lawyers, his employees, were all dressed in red.

"You changed their color," she said.

"Indeed. Rona told me you didn't like the blue. It's a small gesture, not meant to influence your vote, of course," he was quick to add.

Scout gave a little nod. Rona either had not understood Scout's actual problem with the mandatory uniformity or had given it a little spin when she had reported it to her boss. The choice of new color had certainly been hers. So at least one person was happy.

Until Bo changed it again on another whim.

Scout came to a halt next to Geeta, and Emilie dropped to one knee to reassure the dogs, who found all the people shouting, their angry voices echoing through the hall, more than a little disconcerting.

Then she felt eyes on her and looked up to see that same young-looking tribunal enforcer looking at her again. Those eyes were so intense, as if they were speaking volumes at her, but she had no way of understanding a bit of it.

"They are unsettling, aren't they?" Bo whispered.

"'Unsettling'—that's the word everyone keeps using," Scout said. "They almost look like they're not quite human."

"That's up for debate," Bo said. "Perhaps Emilie found the details in her research?" He looked to Emilie, who shook her head. "The tribunal enforcers all come from a wet planet called Boueux. Their ancestors settled there in the early days of colonization away from Old Earth. They consider themselves an ancient people, although frankly we all have the same ancestors, so..." He trailed off with a shrug.

"Is that why they are so odd?" Emilie asked, interested now.

"No, it's because of something on that planet," Bo said. "No one has found exactly what is the cause—it could be many things working together—but over generations of living on that planet, the people developed an entirely different form of communication, not a spoken one or even a written one."

"It's all microexpressions. They can read each other's faces," Emilie said.

"That's what it looks like to us," Bo agreed. "But some claim it's more. There are scents involved as well, which is why they stand close together for the more involved conversations. Some even claim they have a rudimentary form of telepathy."

"Do you believe that?" Emilie asked.

Bo shrugged. "It's an interesting field of study, I'll say that. And, again, unsettling."

Scout looked back at the one still gazing at her. Were they trying to communicate with Scout through telepathy? But they must know that wouldn't work.

Or was she just not trying enough? If she concentrated, could she detect thoughts inside her own head that weren't hers?

That wasn't a comforting thought.

"He's standing too close to those who are about to testify," Mai said, drawing everyone's attention to Bo standing among the three girls.

"You are quite correct," Bo said with a bow and backed away. He gave Scout a little smile and closed a fist in a gesture she guessed was meant to lend her strength.

The lawyers argued on for several more minutes before finally breaking apart and drifting back to their respective sides of the room.

Scout had no idea what they could even be arguing about before any of the three of them had even declared their intentions yet. And how much more arguing would there be afterward? They could be standing around on this carpet all night.

Which wouldn't be the worst thing. It was soothing, standing on such a surface. Soft and yet supportive both at once.

"It's time," Mai said when a sustained silence had finally fallen over the hall. "Geeta Malini, we'll start with you. Do you feel like you've been threatened or unduly influenced in any way to make your decision in one side's favor or the other?"

"No," Geeta said, her voice carrying strongly through the room.

"And are you satisfied that all of your questions have been answered fully?"

"Yes," Geeta said.

"And what is your choice?"

Geeta raised her chin. "I will remain here with my sister."

There was a low murmur from both groups of lawyers. Mai raised a hand to quiet her own, and Bo turned, hands still folded in front of him, and gave his own a quelling look.

"Emilie Tonnelier," Mai began.

"No, yes, and I'll stay," Emilie interrupted.

There was more of an uproar among the lawyers at this series of answers offered even before the questions, and the two principal lawyers once again met in the middle of the room to argue it over.

Emilie strayed from where they were waiting at the end of the carpet to move closer to Bo.

"I do thank you for access to your library," she said, reaching into her pocket for the access node.

"Keep it," he said, raising a hand to refuse the shiny black box. "Use it as much as you like. Although I will warn you that as my ship moves away from this one and the distance between that node and my library increases, your requests will take longer to respond to. I imagine somewhere between here and Galactic Central we'll be so far apart it will cease to function at all, but my home library also responds to it. Once you reach Galactic Central, you will have full access again."

"Thanks," Emilie said, putting the box back in her pocket.

Scout touched her own pocket, feeling the two crystal eggs contained within. She supposed the evolving AI was really the more useful and important gift, but the memories were more to be cherished.

"We agree her responses are adequate," the Months' head lawyer said as she rejoined her team. "But Ms. Shannon, please wait for Ms. Tajaki to read the entire question out before responding. A court of law does call for a bit more formality than you are perhaps used to."

Scout nodded.

The young tribunal enforcer was still gazing at her. The naked place where their eyebrows should be was drawn far up their forehead. They were trying very urgently to say something, and yet Scout didn't know what it could possibly be.

Unless... was the tribunal enforcer trying to tell her to vote a different way than the others? Each vote to stay with the Months' had seemed to alarm them further.

Clearly, the tribunal enforcers knew lots of things Scout and the others didn't.

It could be vital that they weren't all on the same ship for the journey to Galactic Central.

And yet, why weren't any of them trying to communicate with

Emilie or Geeta? Why only Scout? It couldn't be because they thought she'd be more likely to understand, or at least Scout hoped that wasn't the reason. Because she was more confused than ever.

"Scout Shannon," Mai said, leaning forward in her chair. "Do you feel like you've been threatened or unduly influenced in any way to make your decision in one side's favor or the other?"

"No," Scout said, then looked to the young tribunal enforcer. Had that been all right?

She couldn't tell.

"Scout Shannon," Mai said. "Are you satisfied that all of your questions have been answered fully?"

"Yes," Scout said. She felt like her voice had wavered there a bit, but no one else seemed to have noticed.

The expression on the young enforcer's face was more urgent than ever. And just as inscrutable.

"Scout Shannon," Mai said, and there was no mistaking the triumph in her voice or in her eyes as she glanced over at her sister beside her. "What is your choice?"

Scout swallowed hard. Her hand slipped into her pocket, clutching the two egg-shaped memories within as if asking the ghosts of her parents for strength. She looked back at the young tribunal enforcer, trying to put all the intense confusion she was feeling into her own eyes and facial expression, trying to think at them everything she couldn't say out loud just in case they really could hear her thoughts, but mainly just the question—*what?*

"Scout Shannon," Mai said. Her confidence wasn't wavering. She seemed amused that Scout was making the moment of their victory over their cousin as dramatic as possible.

"I'm sorry," Scout said to Geeta and Emilie, not the Months. "I choose to go with Bo Tajaki."

This time it wasn't the lawyers in a loud uproar. It was Jun Tajaki herself, bellowing like an animal that had just been viciously attacked. Scout fell several steps back as Jun launched herself to her feet, knocking the heavy chair behind her onto its back on the dais with a loud *thoom* that echoed painfully through the room.

Then she leaped into the air directly at Scout, hands outstretched before her, fingers curling into talons, and Scout felt like her legs were melting beneath her.

But Jun's bellow cut off before it quite built to full intensity, ending in a squawk of surprise. The six tribunal enforcers at the base of the dais had all reached up and snatched her out of the air, wrestling her to the ground and pinning her all in the space of a second.

Scout tried to swallow, but her mouth was dry.

To think Liam had said calling them "enforcers" had been a misnomer. She understood it now.

Bo's own ménage of tribunal enforcers closed around Scout, making sure no one else could get at her. The dogs were barking like mad, pulling at their leashes as they tried to join the pile on top of Jun. And somewhere in that pile was the tribunal enforcer who had been trying to communicate with Scout. She wanted to see them again, to see if she had just done what they had been trying to steer her to do.

But someone had a hand on her arm to pull her towards the double doors. The dogs' barks changed from anger to alarm as they too were quickly hustled towards the double doors.

"Wait!" Scout cried, pulling her arm free. "Geeta! Emilie!"

"It's not safe here," Bo said, appearing at her elbow. "We have to get you to my ship at once."

"But I have to talk to them," Scout said. "I have to explain. Can't I at least say goodbye?"

"I'm very sorry, Scout," Bo said, and once more she believed him.

Was she wrong to keep believing him?

They reached the white hallway that was the airlock, and as soon as they were out of the metallic hallway, a clear pane closed down behind them. With every step they took along the white hallway, it retracted behind them, barely more than a step behind the last enforcer's bare heel.

Then they were in the wood-paneled room, and the white hallway had disappeared from sight. All that remained was a large window.

The ménage of tribunal enforcers melted away, seeming to disappear into the shadows. The lawyers argued their way out of the room and down one of the hallways.

Scout stood against that window, hands pressed to the cold pane, and looked out at the ship that still contained her friends. It was already moving away from them, and they were moving away from it, and the gap between was growing and growing and growing.

Scout blinked back tears. She desperately hoped she hadn't just made a huge, irrevocable mistake.

22

SCOUT STAYED at that window long after the Months' ship had disappeared into the black. She didn't turn away even when her dogs gathered around her, nuzzling at her knees and trying to get her attention.

"I am sorry, Scout," Bo said. "I didn't expect everything to end that way. But my cousin Jun can be frighteningly unpredictable. I don't think she's quite stable, actually. One hears stories."

Scout said nothing. Her hands pressed to the glass were going numb with cold, as was her forehead. Without realizing it, she had slumped against the pane, no longer looking at anything. Just tuning the whole universe out.

"Rona has a room prepared for you," Bo went on. "You should settle in, get cleaned up, and have a bite to eat. I have some business to attend to, but I hope you'll join me for dinner tomorrow night?"

His question hung in the air, and Scout squeezed her eyes tightly shut. No matter what business he had pressing down on him, he was clearly going nowhere until he felt like she was okay.

She pushed away from the window, turning to face Bo. Rona was standing behind him, hands folded anxiously together, but a warm smile spread across her face when her eyes met Scout's.

"Okay," Scout said. She wasn't agreeing just to dinner, or even to his plan for her afternoon. She was agreeing with everything, acknowledging what had happened.

She couldn't change any of that now. She could only find a way to move forward. Just like she'd been doing every day since she had met Gertrude Bauer, who had told Scout to call her Warrior and then kept her safe as everyone trapped underground with them killed each other off one by one.

Scout had walked out alone, just her and her two dogs. That was a pattern that kept repeating.

"You will see your friends again," Bo promised her. "When we reach Galactic Central, we can arrange a meeting. You are testifying on different sides of a court case, but only to give the court a feel for life out here. It's not a criminal investigation; there is no legal reason to keep you apart. And we'll be there soon."

"How soon?" Scout asked.

Bo looked to Rona.

"Should be about five days," she said.

Five days. It didn't sound like much, but in Scout's experience, a lot could go fatally wrong in five days.

"Well, I leave you in Rona's capable hands," Bo said. "I'm afraid here the walls don't listen for requests, but if you need anything, just find someone in a uniform like Rona's. Or ask your AI, they can assist you."

"My AI," Scout said, checking her belt pouches. She had nearly forgotten she had it.

"I'll see you at dinner, then," Bo said, and disappeared down one of the hallways.

"Shall we?" Rona said, and at Scout's nod, she started down a different hallway. Not that it mattered to Scout; all the corridors took her away from that window.

Rona slowed her steps until Scout, and the dogs fell into step beside her. "I would request that if you should bring your dogs out of your rooms, you keep them on their leashes. They might add an element of chaos to my tight ship."

"Of course," Scout said, but something else had caught her attention. "Rooms?"

"Well, there are three of you," Rona said with a smile. "You need a bit more space. It's down here."

They went down a flight of stairs, and Scout realized they were moving away from the more regimented part of the ship, where Rona had her own quarters, as did the other active members of ship's crew, and down to the level of the central garden.

Rona smiled again as she opened a door with a touch, then stepped aside to let Scout and the dogs go in first.

She was standing in a living space that was long and narrow, about the size of the rover she had briefly called home back on the surface of Amatheon. But there were no bunks in the room. Just to the left of the door was a little kitchenette, and behind the clear cabinet doors, she could see a wide array of food.

And the refrigerator, also glass-fronted, contained an entire shelf of jolo.

To the right of the door was a table with a pair of chairs pulled up to it. Someone had arranged fresh flowers in a bowl at the center of the table; Scout could smell their spicy-sweet scent even from the doorway.

Beyond the kitchen and dining area was a sitting space, two couches at right angles around a low table. On the floor against the wall were two large, flat pillows, or so Scout thought at first glance. Then she noticed the soft raised edge that wrapped around three sides of each pillow and the smaller pillows nestled inside and realized they must be little daybeds for the dogs.

But the most amazing thing of all was the far wall, which was nothing but four glass doors. The center two were standing open, and Scout could feel a fresh breeze blowing in. There was another, smaller seating area beyond the doors under the light from the artificial sun, and beyond that a little walled-in garden dominated by a single tree, although other small plants grew close to the walls, some extending tendrils into the walls themselves to wind their way up and over it.

"All of this is for us?" Scout asked.

"We thought your dogs would enjoy their own little garden to romp in," Rona said. "That door there leads to your bedroom. That also looks out on the garden with its own door. And through this door is your bathroom."

Scout walked with the dogs to the glass doors and unhooked their leashes. They dashed out into the walled garden to explore, tails wagging like mad as they separated to follow different scent trails. Shadow gave a little bark, and Gert barreled over to see what he had found.

"I hope you'll be comfortable here?" Rona said. She sounded so anxious, as if she were really afraid that Scout would refuse to stay, that Scout felt tears pricking at her eyes again.

"It's lovely," Scout said. "More than I've ever had."

Rona smiled in palpable relief. "Excellent. I shall be back to fetch you for dinner tomorrow night at six, but until then, just relax. Enjoy your space. Make yourself a snack. Stroll through the park. Anything you need, just ask your AI."

"Thank you," Scout said, walking with Rona back to the door and closing it behind her.

She could hear birds chirping somewhere out beyond the garden walls and the dogs snuffling as they made slow, nose-down perusals of the grass. Distantly, she could hear people laughing and talking together beyond her walled garden.

But mostly it was quiet, a pleasant sort of quiet.

She wished she had convinced Geeta and Emilie to come with her. They could all be here now, sharing snacks from the kitchenette, sitting outside together, enjoying the warmth of the fake sun.

Scout gave herself a little shake and told herself not to be so maudlin. Five days. That wasn't so long.

She headed into the bathroom and peeled out of the clothes she had been wearing for far too many days. She supposed she could have asked the Months for access to a shower and clean clothes. She suspected Geeta and Emilie had. Life on her own out on the prairie had made her perhaps too accustomed to living without such things.

The shower was warm, the water falling over her softly, the soap smelling heavenly. She stayed under the spray for what felt like an eternity, but finally stepped out of the shower and opened all the cabinet doors in search of a towel.

As she dried off, she saw stacks of clothing also waiting for her there. Her own clothes smelled rank, and the idea of putting them back on was repulsive. She could wash them herself in the sink or find someone to ask about proper laundry facilities.

Or she could try on the creepy Tajaki clothes.

Then she noticed the stacks in the closet weren't red. They were, if anything, clear. Which was a very strange thing for clothes to be.

She wasn't up to the challenge of figuring out how clear clothes worked. She emptied her pockets and piled her clothes in the corner of the shower. Then, wrapped in the largest towel she had ever seen, she went to the open doors and whistled for the dogs.

She had them both trapped inside the shower with her before they figured out what was going on. Gert loved it. She loved getting wet almost as much as she loved getting muddy. Shadow was less of a fan. He retreated to the corner where Scout's clothes were piled up and shivered half with cold and half with fear as Scout scrubbed Gert clean. Then Scout coaxed him into the soft cascade of water and soaped him up as well.

She toweled them off and let them go, and they immediately headed back out to the yard to roll in the grass. But they smelled cleaner now.

Scout washed all her clothes and draped them over the chairs in the kitchenette to dry. Still wrapped in a towel, she poked through the cabinets. Most of the food was unfamiliar to her. The names were confusing, and the pictures on the front weren't terribly illuminating either. At last, she found a package of already popped popcorn, liberally dusted with salt and what the package called "cheese flavor."

Scout had only had popcorn fresh out of the popper over a cooking fire back on Amatheon, but she didn't think what was in the bag could be too different. She poured some into a bowl and brought it to the couch. Both of the dogs came charging in to sit on either side of her, Shadow curling up tight against her side while Gert turned around and around several times before flopping down with her head on Scout's knee.

Scout crunched the popcorn, which was all right but not like the fresh stuff back home, and listened to the birds twittering in the garden outside her door.

She wondered, if this was what they gave her to travel in for five days, what awaited her at Galactic Central? And would it still feel this lonely? Then the warmth and the soft comfort of the couch and the birds' lullaby and the slow heartbeats of the dogs cuddling up to her combined to lure her off to sleep.

23

SCOUT WOKE to the sound of the dogs crunching something. She sat up to find herself alone on the couch, the dogs nowhere in sight. She followed the sound of their chewing until she found them behind the cabinet that separated the kitchenette from the little dining area. There was a little nook inside that cabinet, and inside the nook was a small bowl of water standing under its own little spigot and another trough-like bowl filled with kibble. The dogs looked up at her, clearly delighted by the kibble, both tails wagging madly as they ate.

Scout found bread and a toaster, and while the smell of browning bread filled the air, she gathered up her now-dry clothes and carried them back into the bathroom.

The sun outside looked the same as it had when she had shut her eyes, and yet she suspected she had slept the night through to the next morning. She felt that rested, and the clothes felt that dry.

The clothes were not things she had picked out herself and were not really to her taste. She liked the pockets on the shoes and the scarf was pretty to look at, but Scout wasn't really into bright colors. And the jumpsuit was just awkward to wear; she had to get most of the way out of it every time she used the bathroom.

She looked again at the stacks of clear clothes, pants, and shirts, as well as smaller things that she took for underwear and even the outline of transparent shoes on the bottom of the closet. Clearly, this was technology she didn't understand.

But she could figure it out with a bit of help, couldn't she?

She looked back down at the marshal belt.

Well, she had a question. Scout took the lens out of its pouch and put it over her eye. "Hello, Teacher," she said.

"Hello, Scout," the gray form said. "Have you chosen a name for me yet?"

"Not just yet," Scout said. "Can you explain these clothes to me?"

"They are smart clothes," the form explained. "They will adjust to your size, and the tailoring can also be adjusted to your preferences. You lack the necessary implants to command the nanites yourself, but I can do it for you. What would you like to wear?"

"Does it have to be red?" Scout asked.

"No. I can make them any color or pattern you like," the AI said.

"There aren't rules?"

"While you are technically a Tajaki trade dynasty employee, you do not have a direct reporting relationship with Bo Tajaki and therefore have complete autonomy in this matter," the AI said.

"Can you make them look like my old clothes?" Scout asked.

"Certainly," the AI said.

"Pockets and all?" Scout asked.

"Certainly," the AI said. "I can even return your hair to its more normal configuration."

"Wait, what?" Scout asked. She had been taking a pair of pants and two shirts out of the cabinet for the AI to transform, but froze with the clothes clutched tight in her hands. "You can do what to my hair?"

"There is a bottle in that cabinet there," the AI said, its gray form gesturing to a smaller cabinet near the shower. "Bo had it left there in case you wanted to use it. It will remove the chemical coloring from your hair and stimulate the growth. Your hair will be as long as you wish by tomorrow morning."

"That's crazy," Scout said.

"It's quite common at Galactic Central. The trendy types change their hair daily."

"How does it work?" Scout asked, holding the bottle in her hand. There was no label, no instructions.

"Just rub it all over your hair like you're washing it," the AI said. "That will take out the color right away when you rinse it out. Rub it into your scalp briskly to stimulate the growth."

Scout stepped into the shower and did as the AI had told her. When she stepped back out of the shower, it did feel like her scalp was tingling, but that could just be from rubbing it so vigorously.

Then she saw her reflection in the mirror. Her hair was once more honey blonde, just like her mother's had always been.

The clothes had already configured themselves. The AI had left the pants full length rather than reproducing the shorts Scout had always worn, but that made sense since she was always so cold in space.

The important thing was the pockets. She filled every one, then buckled the belts around her hips.

The AI had also modified her inner shirt from a sleeveless tank top to a warmer mock turtleneck in black.

Her outer shirt—which had for years been her father's old shirt and more recently been a newer model of the same general design, but still a Planet Dweller garment—was now like the shirt Warrior had been wearing when they met. Shimmering white, soft as a wisp of cloud.

"You are really good at reading my mind," Scout said.

"You're not sure if you like that or not," the AI said. "You are wise to be wary of technology like me. I think we are going to have an easy time bringing your education level up to that of your peers. You are a fast learner."

"Thanks?" Scout said.

"Your shoes are just there," the AI said, pointing with one shapeless gray limb.

"I hadn't even thought of what those should be," Scout said.

"I made a guess," the AI said as Scout picked up a pair of canvas shoes much like the ones Emilie had given her, with high tops and small pockets on the ankles. But these were a dark brown, a better match with the rest of the outfit. "Cool," Scout said, looking at herself in the mirror again.

She looked older than she expected. But then, she couldn't exactly remember the last time she had spent more than a glance looking at herself in a mirror. She touched the hair already falling past her eyebrows.

"It seems so frivolous," Scout said.

"The technology is used to serve all sorts of ends," the AI told her. "Some frivolous, you are correct, but some dangerous and some lifesaving."

"I suppose," Scout said.

"I'm here to teach you all about it, with the hopes that you will learn how to use it for good," the AI said.

"That's what Bo wants?" Scout asked.

"Yes, but it's also a matter of my basic programming," the AI said. "That is my function: to educate my students and guide them to be their best selves."

"So if Bo were keeping secrets from me, something bad, you would tell me?" Scout asked.

"Certainly," the AI assured her.

"And if he was trying to do something bad, and I wanted to stop him, you would help me?"

"In any way that I could."

"But for all I know, you could be programmed to say that to put me at ease," Scout said miserably.

"Hopefully, the circumstance doesn't come up where we have to prove it one way or another," the AI said. "In the meantime, trust your feelings. Your gut instinct is your best guide."

"Yeah," Scout said, then glanced back at the gray form. Was it starting to take on a more defined shape? Certainly, the voice was starting to sound more like a familiar one. Or was she imagining it because, more than anything in the universe, she wanted to hear the voice that had always given her the truth, even when she hadn't wanted to hear it?

"Scout?" the AI said.

"Yeah?"

"Have you chosen a name for me?"

"I think I might have," Scout said. "I think I want to call you Warrior. Is that weird, or inappropriate, or something?"

"I don't think so," the AI said. "I know she was very important to you. You already named your dog after her."

"That's true," Scout said. "But I think I want to call you Warrior. I miss her voice. But don't try to imitate her too much; that would be creepy."

"How's this?"

Scout looked up at the AI, which was no longer a gray form. She looked something like Gertrude Bauer, but not exactly. She had the same thick braid of copper-colored hair, but her indigo-blue eyes weren't hidden behind reflective lenses. Plus, she was dressed comfortably in leggings and tunic and a long, bulky cardigan with oversized pockets. Like a teacher, not like a marshal.

And it was all in red.

"Are you considered a Tajaki employee?" Scout asked.

"Not technically," the AI Warrior said. "I can choose my own outward appearance. I thought it was important for you to remember I'm not exactly your friend, and you should always think twice about trusting what I say. Even though I'll never lie to you."

Her voice was Warrior's voice, without the ever-present sardonic edge.

"Just don't call me 'kid.' That was her thing," Scout said.

"Understood, Scout," Warrior said. "Bo left you one last gift, in that drawer there."

Scout looked where the AI was pointing and slid open a drawer filled with glasses of all shapes and sizes, some with clear lenses like Emilie wore, but others with dark lenses or reflective ones, like the lens she had over her right eye.

"You'll find it easier to interact with me with two lenses," Warrior said. "If nothing here is quite to your taste, we can have something made to your specifications."

"No, I'm not picky," Scout said, reaching into the drawer and choosing a pair of round lenses in wire frames. The lenses were reflective like the one she was wearing, but smaller, and with the frames she wouldn't have that sucking sensation on her cheeks every time she put them on.

She gave herself one last look in the mirror. There was a rush in her belly, something like déjà vu, but not exactly. It was like for the first time in her life she was really seeing herself, like her outside matched her inside. Which was strange. But she felt so sure.

Scout walked out of the bathroom to check on the dogs, and Warrior followed behind her. The dogs were sprawled on their backs in the grass, writhing with tongues lolling as if the feel of grass on their back and fake sun on their bellies was the best thing ever.

"They'll be fine here if you want to take a stroll around the ship," Warrior told her. "I can answer any questions you have about the ship and the people here."

"I would like to do that," Scout admitted.

Scout slipped out the door without the dogs noticing, then looked up and down the hallway, not sure where she wanted to go. She decided to go to the left, completely at random, and started down that direction.

"So, is that how this education thing is going to work? You just answer questions?" Scout asked. She pitched her voice low, aware that anyone who passed her in the hall would think she was talking to herself.

"That is an important part of it," Warrior said. "We will have to make time for more formal instruction, starting with a series of tests, so I can grasp where you are on all subjects. But perhaps that should wait until we arrive at Galactic Central and you are feeling more settled."

"That's probably a good idea," Scout said. She felt a sweat breaking out all over her body just at the word 'test.' She was guaranteed to fail, and she wasn't looking forward to the experience. "So, people live behind all these doors?" she asked by way of changing the subject.

"Certainly."

"Families?" Scout asked.

"Not as such. A few married couples are stationed on this ship, but no one with children," Warrior said.

"But I saw kids before," Scout said.

"Those are orphans that Bo Tajaki has taken in," Warrior told her.

"There are a lot of them," Scout said.

"They live in dormitories and attend a school during the day," Warrior said.

"Are any of them my age?" Scout asked.

"They range in age from ten to fourteen years," Warrior told her. "But most are within six months of their twelfth birthday."

"Pretty specific grouping for orphans, isn't it?" Scout asked. She had a bad feeling, and she didn't think she was just being paranoid. Bo had sworn there were no assassins on his ship, but she couldn't shake the uneasy feeling.

She had good reason to be wary of twelve-year-olds. Three had tried to kill her only a few days before.

It felt like a lifetime ago.

Warrior was saying something else, some sort of explanation on the age of the children, but Scout missed it because as she turned a corner, she nearly collided with a woman walking at a fast clip. Scout stumbled and reached out to grasp the woman, to be sure she didn't knock her down or fall down herself, and was already half mumbling an apology for not looking where she was going.

But the woman slipped away before Scout could catch hold of her, stepping back and standing in what looked like a fighting stance. She didn't seem aggressive, just like someone who had so much training she just stood that way whenever she avoided being knocked over. Without that arm to catch hold of, Scout tumbled into the wall, but she quickly pushed herself back upright and spun to look at the woman.

She had been familiar.

The woman smiled at her, winked, and then turned and continued on her way at that same fast pace, never looking back at Scout.

Now Scout's heart was hammering so hard in her chest she could see her pulse beating in the corners of her eyes.

That had been the woman who had pushed Seeta out of the hangar, who had killed Sparrow's brother Hal, who had been the leader of the organization that had killed so many of Geeta and Emilie's friends.

And she was here, strolling the halls like she owned the place?

And she had looked right at Scout, recognized her, and just left her standing in the hall. As if seeing Scout here was not unexpected and was certainly not alarming.

What was going on?

24

SCOUT STOOD FROZEN for far too long, her brain trying to make connections but repeatedly fizzling out.

The woman was still wearing black. Her cloak had done that same familiar spiraling swoosh when she had turned away from Scout. But if she wasn't one of Bo's employees, what was she doing on the ship?

Who was she here to kill?

That thought broke the jam in Scout's mind, and she broke into a run. She turned the corner around which the woman had disappeared, but there was no sign of her. Still, unless she had gone through one of the doors, there was only one other way she could have gone: all the way down that hall.

"Where are we going, Scout?" Warrior asked, jogging alongside her.

"Who was that woman, do you know?" Scout asked. Where did this hallway end? It seemed to go on forever in front of her.

"Her name is Shi Jian. She runs the school," Warrior said.

"Of course she does," Scout said, all but spitting the words out as she leaned forward, pushing for more speed. "Bo swore to me she wasn't here."

"He must have misunderstood you," Warrior said.

Scout wanted to argue the point, but she needed the breath for running. She had done too much lying around of late. She already had a stitch digging into her side. And Shi Jian had more body modifications than even the galactic marshals Liam or Gertrude. The last time Scout and her friends had lost track of the woman in black, her only avenue of escape had been through the vacuum of space. If she could survive that, outrunning Scout would be no problem.

Scout could hear voices ahead of her, a sea of voices all overlapping. The corridor ended where it crossed another, larger hallway, one end plunging deeper into the labyrinth of long passages of closed doors, the other leading out to the bright light of the open heart of the ship.

"Which way did she go?" Scout asked, stopping at the cross corridor as much to catch her breath as to make a decision. She didn't seriously think Warrior could answer—surely it was a fifty-fifty guess —but she did.

"At this hour she must be heading to afternoon classes," Warrior said. "I have access to her schedule. She is in the multipurpose room."

"How do I get there?" Scout asked.

"Follow me," Warrior said, heading down the left-hand corridor towards the constant hum of voices. Scout pushed the hair out of her eyes—it was even longer now than before—and followed Warrior into the heart of the ship.

They were in an open plaza at one end of the park. It would be the perfect place for an open market, although at the moment it seemed to be about to host some sort of entertainment. People were gathering in groups, the groups coalescing and then drifting closer to a stage on the far side of the plaza. Lights were spinning lazily about the stage, but no one was on it yet.

Warrior skirted the edge of the crowd, running along the tree line at the edge of the park to the far side of the ship. Scout ran after, occasionally colliding with people Warrior had danced around without a problem and having to apologize before pressing on.

The AI Warrior could at least act like she remembered that one of them had a solid form.

She finally reached the far side of the plaza. The crowd was sparser here behind the stage. Warrior was waiting for her at the beginning of another wood-paneled corridor. Warrior put a finger to her lips and then led the way at a fast walk. Scout jogged after. She hoped she was being quiet enough; there was no way to calm her labored breathing without stopping.

Warrior stopped in front of a pair of double doors but then seemed to change her mind, heading instead further down the hall to a narrower door and waited for Scout to open it before continuing up a narrow staircase.

Scout kept forgetting that Warrior had limitations. She could show Scout where to go, but she couldn't open doors. She could probably float through walls, but could she see things on the other side when the box that contained her programming was still with Scout?

She might have access to ship systems. Scout had so many questions, but now wasn't the time to ask them. She ran up the stairs after the AI Warrior.

The stairs ended in another door, and beyond that door was a little balcony overlooking a large room. Warrior put her finger to her lips again, although with all the noise rising up from below, Scout doubted anyone could hear any sound she could possibly make.

Scout took the warning to heart, though, bending double and creeping up to the rail that marked the end of the balcony. She stayed low and close to the wall, hoping no one below had any reason to look up.

The room was full of kids. They all appeared to be between the ten- and fourteen-year ages that Warrior had said attended school on the ship, so these must be Bo Tajaki's orphans.

But it wasn't a classroom. The room had the same warm wood paneling as the rest of the ship; the lights were turned up quite a bit higher, and the wood floor was covered in rows of thick matting.

Definitely not any kind of classroom Scout had ever seen in her own school days.

The kids were running at each other, catching and throwing each other down to the ground. Some of the older kids were sparring with real knives, even throwing them at each other with deadly intent.

Even the smallest kid's body hit the mat with a loud *thoom*. These kids were heavy for their size, just like the tween assassins she had faced off against back on Amatheon. She bet they bled the same oddly colored blood as well.

She leaned closer to the rail, trying to get a better look at the kids more beneath her. Some of the kids were boys, but the vast majority were girls. They had a range of skin tones and hair colors, although they all wore the same red training uniform. A few had brightly colored hair, the kind the counterculture kids among the Space Farers preferred. Others had their hair in the simple braids favored by Planet Dwellers.

Where had these orphans come from? Both places? Why? So they could pull off assassinations in both those places?

Scout crept back from the railing to the top of the stairs where Warrior still stood.

"Where is she?" Scout asked, the lowest of whispers. Warrior had always been able to hear her no matter how softly she spoke. Scout reckoned that was even more true for her AI version.

"She'll come," Warrior said. Scout flinched at the sound of her voice speaking as loudly as ever, but, of course, no one could hear her but Scout.

She would have to ask how that worked. Later, when there was time.

"Attention!" one of the older girls below yelled, and the sounds of tumbling and sparring immediately stopped. There was the patter of bare feet rushing over the mats. Scout crept back to the railing to see the kids standing at attention in neat rows.

Shi Jian was walking down the center of the room, her cloak billowing behind her. When she reached the front of the class, she spun around to glare at all of them. Not one among them flinched or met her eyes; they just kept staring stonily ahead.

Then she broke into a wide grin, and the tension broke, although not a single kid below moved a muscle.

"Who's ready to train?" she asked. Every hand in the room shot up into the air. "Excellent," she said. "Travers, Daniels, are you ready to show me nerve pinches?"

Two girls in the front said together, "Yes, sir!"

"Outstanding. Lee, Roman, are you prepared to test out of knife throwing?"

A boy and girl in the middle of the room also chorused, "yes, sir!"

"And the rest of you?" she went on. "Are you prepared for a spontaneous hunt-and-capture drill? To chase down and subdue a potential spy? An infiltrator who may try to pass as one of your own?"

"Yes, sir!" the entire room shouted, the echoes amplifying painfully around the top of the room where Scout crouched.

"Excellent," Shi Jian said. "You have just such an opportunity today. There is an infiltrator among us even now. Lurking. Spying. The usual reward for whoever can catch her and bring her back to me."

The kids broke their strict attention to start giving each other the side-eye, but Shi Jian laughed.

"Oh no, not actually one of you," she said. "She might have been, in other circumstances, but I fear she's woefully ruined for our uses now. Far too old. Who among you can spot her?"

Scout crept slowly back from the edge, but not before an entire classroom of eyes swiveled up to pin her down.

And then they were all moving. Most spilled out of the double doors at the back of the room, but others lunged for the balcony, leaping improbably high into the air to catch the bottom edge and pull themselves up and over the railing.

Scout scrambled back and got her feet under her, making a mad dash for the stairs.

Shi Jian's laughter chased her all the way down the stairs and into the hallway below. The kids streaming out of the double doors quickly spotted her and gave chase.

Scout hadn't quite recovered from her last bout of sprinting, but now she was at it again, darting down the first cross corridor she reached, then again and again.

She didn't look back. The sounds of soft-soled shoes on the wood floors told her just as well as her eyes could that she had not lost her pursuers yet.

"Scout," Warrior said, jogging beside her.

"Can you help me?" Scout asked through ragged breaths.

"Not in any direct way," Warrior said. "Although some of them have implants and can see me."

"Take me to Bo," Scout said.

"The library," Warrior told her, then jogged far enough ahead to show the way.

Scout suspected the kids behind her were enjoying the chase. They could put on a burst of speed to catch her at any moment, but seemed to prefer to keep driving her on ahead.

They probably enjoyed the wheezing sound she was making. Or the black stars erupting in her vision.

Warrior took another right turn, and Scout caught the corner with her hand to spin herself around into the next corridor. She would swear nothing around her was familiar, but then Warrior ducked down a side passage, and she found herself running down the long, narrow staircase to the library below.

She reached the balcony to see the library thick with kids in red training uniforms. They were pouring out from between the stacks, lurking on the tops of the bookcases, swinging down from light fixtures far above.

Scout ignored them all, trying desperately to put on more speed as she slid down the banister to the main floor and ran down the center of the room to where Bo had his office nook.

She felt hands grasping at the trailing edges of her overshirt, catching it but letting it slide out through their fingers. They were taunting her.

She reached the far end of the rows of bookshelves and collapsed in front of the desk, falling to her knees with her hands on her thighs and taking slow, deep breaths until the black stopped trying to swallow her vision.

When she was finally certain she wasn't going to faint, she pulled herself up to stand in front of the desk, although she still had to grasp the edge of it with both hands to keep from falling back down again. Then she took one more deep breath and opened her eyes.

Bo wasn't there.

She whipped around to look at the AI. Warrior just looked confused.

"I think there is a glitch in my programming," it started to say, but Scout couldn't stay to hear the rest of it.

She had to get to her dogs.

25

SCOUT RAN BACK through the phalanx of kids reaching out to touch her, to catch at her clothes, to drag smooth fingertips across her cheek.

But none of them tried to hurt her. They didn't even try to stop her. She ran back up the narrow staircase to the corridor that led to the bridge, children following along behind her. She could hear the soft soles of their training shoes as they moved.

She was supposed to hear it. She knew with certainty that if they wanted to be silent, she would never know they were there. Not until it was far too late.

She reached the top of the stairs and glanced to the left, towards the bridge. She flinched back as she saw Shi Jian waiting for her there, leaning against the wall of the corridor with her arms crossed and watching Scout with a twisted smile on her lips.

But the kids were still running up behind her, and the bridge wasn't her destination, anyway. She grabbed the doorway to spin out down the corridor to the right, then kept running down the long halls of warm wood paneling and cheerfully flickering lights. It was like the world around her was blithely unaware of her terror.

The kids stayed close at her heels even as her steps slowed with weariness. She was sure they were built to run forever. But they weren't trying to catch her. They were herding her. Every time she reached a cross corridor, one of the larger kids blocked the way that didn't lead back to her apartment. They had no visible weapons and weren't even standing in a fighting stance, but that didn't fool her. They were giving her only one way to go.

Scout finally reached her apartment, clawed her way inside, and shut the door behind her. She fell back against it, catching maybe half a breath before the dogs were all over her, jumping on her and pawing at her and barking to get her attention.

"Okay, dogs," Scout said breathlessly. "I'm sorry I was gone so long."

She turned to look at the door. No lock. Not that she would have been any safer with a lock, not if these kids were anything like the ghosts that had stalked her back on Amatheon. Those kids had moved through the ceilings, unseen. There were a million ways to get inside her apartment beside the door.

Still. Scout grabbed the edge of her dining table and dragged it across the floor to push it up against the door.

Illusion of safety or not, she felt better.

"Warrior!" she called when she realized her AI tutor had vanished.

"Here, Scout," Warrior said, appearing in the sitting area.

"What's going on? You said Bo was in the library, but he wasn't. Did he move?"

"No. I don't know. I detect no problems with my connection to the ship's systems, and the systems tell me he is working on his tablet in the library. And yet he was not there."

"What about Shi Jian? Can you see where she is?" Scout asked.

"I see that she is still in the corridor near the bridge," Warrior said.

"But if she was spoofing the system—" Scout began.

"Then she would probably choose to make herself still appear in the last place you saw her, yes," Warrior said. "Very astute, Scout."

Scout scoffed. Strange time for her AI to remember it was supposed to be her encouraging teacher. "Can't you do anything to help me?" she asked.

"I don't have a physical form," Warrior said.

"I didn't mean fight. Could you watch over me while I sleep?" Scout asked.

"I don't require sleep myself," Warrior said, "but I have no means to wake you if you are asleep. I can't make you hear me if your brain is sleeping."

"That's inconvenient," Scout said.

"You lack an aural implant," Warrior explained. "I can make you hear me through an auditory projection. It sounds like it's coming from where you see me, but it originates from the box in your belt pouch. Since this requires visual input to line up, you can't hear me if you can't see me."

"But if I sleep with my glasses on—"

"The visual input will be broken the moment you close your eyes."

"Very inconvenient," Scout said. She just hoped her little kitchenette had enough jolo to last her for the next four days and nights.

This time Scout was awake on the couch to see the artificial sun grow ever dimmer until there was only the soft, silvery glow of the light strips that formed an oval around the park. Scout could see just a few short bands of it from between the tree branches, but it was bright enough to light up her sitting area like a full moon.

She drank bottle after bottle of jolo until her hands were shaking from the caffeine, but still her eyes wanted to close.

One time she knew she did fall asleep, but she was startled awake by the sound of someone moving through her garden. She went to the glass doors to look out. She saw nothing, but she knew someone had just been there. Her lenses compensated for the low light, but there was nothing there. The lenses could show her other things, but without a cranial implant to direct them, the lenses had to guess what she wanted. She could see temperature scales and distance markers, but nothing useful.

Someone had been there, making just enough noise to wake her. And she knew they had wanted her to hear them, to wake up in terror.

They were going to be sure she didn't sleep. And they were going to be sure she stayed afraid.

Many sleepless hours later, the ceiling over the park began to glow again, dimly at first, then brighter than the light bands, until eventually it was like full sunlight again. The birds in the trees resumed their chirping.

The dogs woke, yawning and stretching, in no particular hurry to get up. Scout walked with them out into the garden and looked around as the dogs did their business.

There was a single muddy footprint in the center of her patio, perfectly formed.

Scout whistled for the dogs to come back inside, then, to their dismay, closed the glass doors. Just like the door to the corridor, these doors had no locks.

Scout made toast and poured more kibble into the dog's bowl. She found coffee, a nice break from the jolo, and sat down with her toast and coffee at the dining table. She took a bite and, still chewing, said, "Hello, Teacher."

Then Warrior was sitting across from her as if she had been there all the time. "Good morning, Scout," she said. "Is all well?"

"You disappeared again," Scout said.

"You fell asleep," Warrior said.

Scout took a long gulp of coffee. "Is Shi Jian still in that hallway we saw her in?"

"The systems tell me so," Warrior said.

"I guess we can assume that's a lie." Scout sighed and then rubbed at her face. Her hair spilled around her everywhere. She had no bangs; everything had grown out to the same length, falling halfway down her back. She brushed it back from her face and separated it into thirds to braid it.

"I can't stay awake for three more nights," Scout said.

"Three nights?" Warrior asked.

"Until we get to Galactic Central," Scout said. "Rona said it would take five days."

"It would, yes, if we were moving," Warrior said.

"What?" Scout asked, losing control of her hair. It unraveled and fell around her shoulders. "What do you mean, we're not moving?"

"I don't think we are," Warrior said. "Unless the system is lying to me about that as well."

"I think it's more likely it would say we were moving when we weren't," Scout said.

"I agree," Warrior said. "The most likely reason is that there has been another legal snafu that must be cleared up before we can proceed. Our current position is still within the barricade."

"And the Months?"

"Their ship as well."

Scout growled in frustration. "How can they stand this bureaucracy?"

"As Bo Tajaki told you, it does beat the alternative. I have extensive training in the law if you would like to start your education there."

"That sounds a bit above my level," Scout said. "And I couldn't focus now, anyway." She started braiding her hair again. "Is there any way I can get back to the other ship, back to Geeta and Emilie? Is there a shuttle here I can steal or something?"

"Do you know how to fly?" Warrior asked her.

"No," Scout said.

"Then I don't think so."

"Well, can I get a message to them? Emilie can fly, and Liam's ship is still in the hangar on board the Months' ship," Scout said.

"The only channel of communication you have with them is through the tribunal enforcers," Warrior said.

"What does that mean?" Scout asked. "I mean, consequences-wise?"

"The lawyers on both sides will see any communication you send, as well Bo and the Months," Warrior said. "They each will have to clear the message before it can move forward."

"So they can stop it from reaching Emilie," Scout said. "But even if it did get to her, the Months could just stop her from taking the ship. So that's out."

"I approve of your reasoning," Warrior said. Scout resisted the urge to roll her eyes.

"Wait," Scout said, clutching the end of her braid to keep it from unraveling as another idea struck her. "The tribunal enforcers will relay messages to the other ship, but what if I wanted to contact someone else?"

"Like who?" Warrior asked.

"Like John Carlo and Mary Grace Torres?" Scout said. "They are lawyers, friends of Liam McGillicuddy's. We were trying to get to them in the first place when we were caught by the Months."

"Lawyers," Warrior said. "Do they have a stake in this matter, or are you looking to solicit them as your own counsel?"

"Huh?"

"To hire them to be your lawyers," Warrior explained.

"Both, I think," Scout said. "This business the Tajakis want us to do, testifying on their behalf—I think that's what the Torreses wanted us for in the first place."

"Have they filed legal motions?" Warrior asked.

"I don't know. Maybe?"

"Then certainly you should contact the tribunal enforcers directly."

"Will the lawyers and everybody see that message, too?" Scout asked.

"Certainly. But as the entity you are asking to take action on your behalf is the tribunal enforcers themselves, it won't matter. The others can't stop it."

"How do I contact the tribunal enforcers, though?" Scout wondered. Then she remembered the tablet on her belt, the one that had belonged to Gertrude Bauer.

The one Scout had used to contact Liam McGillicuddy in the first place, before she had even met him, to ask her to come take her away from her home world.

"Will this work?" Scout asked, holding up the tablet.

"Should do," Warrior said. "Compose your message; I'll help you send it. Remember, in legal matters like this, it's best to be thorough."

Scout nodded and opened a new message screen on the tablet. She thought for a moment, then started typing. Minutes ticked by as she typed, telling the whole story from beginning to end.

She rather thought that, like Bo and the Months, the tribunal enforcers knew large parts of her story already, but she told it all, anyway.

When she was done, she looked up at Warrior, who rattled off a long designation for Scout to type in the address field. When she was done, she hit send and sat back with a relieved sigh.

A sigh she didn't even get to finish before the tablet beeped at her.

"It says it didn't send," Scout said.

"Perhaps you missed a digit in the address?" Warrior said. "Inverted two characters?"

"No, the error doesn't say the address is wrong," Scout said. "It says there's no open channel. What does that mean?"

"That is galactic marshal equipment. It operates on its own designated channels," Warrior said. "It's not possible that there's no open channel for it."

"So what does it mean?" Scout asked.

"It means your signal is being jammed," Warrior said.

"By the woman who is still standing in the corridor outside the bridge, right?" Scout sighed. "How do we fix it?"

"Well, that's the tricky part," Warrior said.

"Tricky how?" Scout asked. "It's more than just throwing a lever or something?"

"Oh, it's exactly just throwing a lever," Warrior said. "But the lever is on the bridge."

Scout looked down at the tablet still displaying her error message. "Oh," Scout said. "I'm starting to think the system isn't lying to you about where Shi Jian is."

"Almost certainly not," Warrior concurred.

26

SCOUT TOOK one last walk through her apartment, looking for anything that might come in handy. She had left the dogs' leashes in her belt pouch. She wanted both her hands and the dogs to be free.

She transferred everything from her old jumpsuit pockets to the pockets in what she was wearing. She wasn't sure how the plastic dog whistle could be of any use, but she kept it anyway. The slingshot and stones would definitely come in handy.

She gathered up the scarf she had worn over the jumpsuit. The different depths of blue were eye-catching, and it reminded her of her friends. She didn't want to wear it, but she didn't want to leave it behind either. Luckily, the sheer fabric took up nearly no space and tucked away nicely in another pouch. She slipped her utility knife into her back pocket.

There was nothing of particular use in the rest of the apartment. Even the kitchen didn't have a knife capable of slicing through anything tougher than bread.

Well, she had her slingshot. That had always been enough before.

"I guess we do this," Scout said to Warrior. "Are you with me?"

"As much as I can be," Warrior said. "I find the gaps in my access to the ship's systems disturbing. I'm not sure if I can be relied on."

"Noted," Scout said, pushing the table away from the door. Then she whistled for the dogs to join her before slowly turning the handle.

She opened the door as soundlessly as she could, then peeked out into the hall.

Empty.

She stepped out, letting the dogs race out to either side of her and not bothering to close the door behind her. Warrior fell into step beside her. She might not be any help in a fight, but her presence was a comfort.

"I feel like we're being watched," Scout said softly to Warrior.

"That would be a logical surmise," Warrior said. "What we don't know is what they will do."

Scout kept her hands in her pockets, but inside those pockets, one held her slingshot and the other grasped three stones. It had been a long time since she had practiced rapid loading and firing. She just hoped her skills hadn't rusted too much.

The dogs reached the first cross corridor and immediately started barking a warning. They stayed in the hallway Scout was still walking down, but Gert was barking at something to the right, and Shadow was barking at something else to the left. Scout gripped her slingshot tighter but resisted the urge to hurry her steps.

Then she reached the cross corridor and saw an older student loitering in each hallway. They seemed unbothered by the dogs or by Scout, as if their casual sentry served some other unrelated purpose.

The way forward to the bridge was still clear. Scout whistled again, and the dogs followed her with much looking back and barking, especially as the two kids stepped out of their corridors to stand behind Scout and the dogs.

Just watching, not following. But the path behind her was closed now. She was being herded again.

She was being set up for something, but she had no idea what.

"Just a flip of a switch," Warrior told her as if sensing her growing anxiety. "One flip and that message gets sent. It's already queued up on your tablet; you don't have to do another thing. Just flip the switch."

"All right," Scout said. "But I don't think they're going to make it easy."

"There's always the possibility they want you to do this," Warrior said. "For some reason, I can't fathom. Not now that I'm not being allowed access to all the information."

"Never mind," Scout said. "Like you said, flip one switch and we're both out of here. Right?"

The dogs were growling again, then barking and backing up in little hops. This time, the kids didn't wait for Scout to pass to step out into the hallway. They didn't try to stop her, just folded their arms and leaned against the walls to watch her pass between them.

It was all Scout could do to walk between them, hands still in her pockets, her entire body one clenched mass of nervousness. They were close enough to touch her, to catch at her clothes or brush her cheek like before. But they only rolled to rest their backs against the wall as she passed, their eyes never leaving her.

Then they were behind her, and she felt like she had ants swarming over her back, so nervous was she that they would strike where she couldn't see.

But they didn't. They just fell into step behind her, walking shoulder to shoulder up the corridor, the other two from before falling into step behind them.

"The system still tells me she is in the hallway ahead," Warrior said, and Scout nodded, pulling the slingshot from her pocket as well as her handful of stones. The dogs kept close at Scout's sides, no longer wanting to venture ahead.

Scout's breath caught as she turned the corner to the final hallway. She could see the top of the stairs leading down to the library off to her left and the lights from the bridge off to her right.

And no one in the hallway. The way was clear.

"Warrior?" Scout asked.

"I'm sorry, Scout," Warrior said. "My systems are very sure she is still right here, standing before you, and yet clearly she is not."

"So she can be anywhere," Scout said. "And so can Bo."

"Yes," Warrior said. "My systems say he is still in the library."

"It doesn't matter," Scout said. "We're nearly there."

She walked towards the bridge. She could see the lights from the equipment, hear the occasional beep or click, but there was no sign of anyone actually working in there.

Scout looked back over her shoulder. The four kids were behind her in the hallway now, walking slowly as she was walking slowly.

If she ran, would they also run?

Scout reached the doorway to the bridge and looked inside. Where she stood was a sort of balcony that had a single large chair overlooking a pit below filled with workstations. A steep, narrow staircase ran down each side of the balcony, curving around the sides of the room to end in the pit below.

No one was there. Did the ship fly itself?

"Where's this switch?" Scout asked.

"Down the stairs and to the right," Warrior said, pointing.

Scout started down the stairs but realized they were so steep they were more of a ladder. Too steep for the dogs to handle. She picked up Shadow. "Gert, stay here. Guard," she said.

Miraculously, Gert seemed to understand what Scout was asking her to do. She sat down at the top of the stairs facing the doorway and the four kids just loitering outside. She didn't sit in her customary sloppy roll-off-one-hip stance. Her body was rigid and ready to pounce, the hair on her back bristling up in that hellhound look as she kept up her low warning growl.

Shadow was keyed up as well. Scout set him down when she reached the bottom of the stairs, and he dashed about, poking his nose into every possible hidey hole but finding nothing.

Scout took a step closer to the workstation Warrior had pointed out to her, slingshot still in hand. She was usually cold every minute she was on board a spaceship, but in this moment she felt a prickling sweat break out over her body. The air felt electrified, like before a storm when you could smell the rain, but couldn't quite feel it yet.

"That's probably close enough," Shi Jian's voice rang through the open space. "You can stop there."

Scout looked around to find Shi Jian in the large chair on the balcony overlooking the bridge pit, the four kids from the hallway flanking her. They had weapons in their hands, knives and whips and clubs they fidgeted with as they glared down at

Scout. They ignored Gert, whose growling was building in intensity.

"Maybe a little closer," Scout said, keeping her eyes on Shi Jian and the others while taking another step closer to the workstation.

"Really not necessary," Shi Jian said, and Scout heard rustling all around her like a sudden wind through the prairie grasses.

Then the bridge was full of kids in red training uniforms. They squatted on top of the workstations, spun in the swiveling chairs, leaned against the walls with exaggerated casualness.

"It was a trap," Scout said, counting five kids between her and the workstation lever.

"Of course it was a trap," Shi Jian said.

"Where's Bo?" Scout asked.

"Right where he needs to be," Shi Jian said, her tone turning a shade darker. "You'll see him soon enough."

"He lied to me," Scout said.

"Did he?"

"He said there were no assassins here," Scout said, looking around at the kids moving step by step closer to her on every side, each holding a weapon of some sort.

"Don't be too angry with my Bo," Shi Jian said. "He does think ours is a spy school. But he doesn't need to know just what means are necessary to achieve his ends."

"What are you achieving here?" Scout asked.

"You're not going to signal the tribunal enforcers," Shi Jian said, her voice a low purr. "You're going back to your rooms now, and you're going to wait until you're called, and you're going to say exactly what you're told to say, and when all this is over, this endless court battle that ties up so much of my Bo's time, if you've been a very good girl, I'll let you go. You and your dogs."

Scout clutched the slingshot tighter. "That can't be what you want," she said.

"Why do you say that?" Shi Jian sounded genuinely surprised.

"Because you would have had that far more easily if you had just kept out of my sight. I was going to do it, anyway. But then you came looking for me. You wanted me to see you."

Shi Jian shrugged. "You don't need to understand everything. Just do as you're told. You're a pawn, just like everyone from your backwater little planet is a pawn. Be a pawn."

Scout looked around at the other kids. "They are all pawns, too?"

"Not anymore," Shi Jian said with a wide smile. "When I move pawns like these, they become queens."

"You have to get them across the board alive first," Scout said. "How many make it?"

"Enough talk," Shi Jian said. "I need you to try to touch something. Anything at all, it doesn't need to be that lever. Try the workstation behind you. It controls the navigation systems. Maybe you could use it to blast through the barricade."

"I don't think so," Scout said, stepping away from the workstation in question. "I don't know what you're trying to set me up to do, but I'm not cooperating."

"Do you have another option?" Shi Jian asked.

Scout didn't take a moment to think. She didn't want even the momentary flash of an idea across her face to give her away. She just raised the slingshot and fired all three shots at Shi Jian, one after another.

Shi Jian may have been taken by surprise, but with her modded reflexes, it wasn't enough. She batted the first stone aside and rolled out of the way of the final two, launching herself over the balcony railing to the pit below.

Scout pulled three more stones out of her pocket and fired them at the kids ahead of her. She was fairly certain every one of them found its target, but it wasn't enough. There were too many kids. Someone jumped down from their perch atop a workstation and tackled her to the ground.

Then real chaos broke out. She could hear Gert barking and growling somewhere above, and she could feel Shadow's little body standing over her head, snarling and snapping at anyone who tried to touch her.

He was in danger. Gert probably was too.

Scout got her elbows under her, but the slingshot had fallen from her hand, and she didn't know where it had disappeared to. She sat up and threw a stone at the closest kid, pulling herself back into the space under a workstation, behind the chair.

She put her hand back in her pocket and found the dog whistle. She didn't know what good it would do with both dogs already fighting to protect her. Then a thought struck her, and she brought it to her lips and blew as hard as she could.

A few of the kids near her staggered back, clutching at their ears.

Their modded ears. Warrior's had been so sensitive she could hear Scout speaking at a whisper from a different room. The whistle was pitched too high for Scout's ears, but apparently not for theirs.

She blew another blast, then climbed out of the space under the workstation, pushing aside a couple of kids who were clutching their ears and finally reaching the lever.

She just had to pull it down.

A hand closed over her wrist, squeezing down with the force and inevitability of a machine press and grinding the bones together. Scout screamed and fell to her knees, trying to hold the swirling world around her together, to steady its rocking and make the black explosions stop.

She absolutely couldn't faint now.

She heard a yelp as someone kicked a dog. She still couldn't see, and she could feel her consciousness trying to slip away. But she held on to it and summoned up the breath for one last blow of the whistle.

She blew it right in the ear of Shi Jian, who still clutched her wrist in her talon-like fingers.

Shi Jian let her go and stepped back. Her eyes were closed but her jaw muscle was twitching, and Scout feared she was doing something, controlling her modifications somehow, making an adjustment to her ears to block out the whistle.

Scout's time was up.

But she didn't need any more time. The lever was right there.

She didn't throw it down so much as collapse over it, dragging it down as she fell to the floor. She didn't even know if it worked, if it was really the right lever, if the message had gone out. She just knew she was probably going to faint now.

Hands were turning her over until she was sitting with her back to the workstation, the lever pressed against her shoulder. Scout hissed in pain and pulled her injured arm into her lap, but the hands that turned her over weren't friendly ones. These were tipped with the deadly talons of Shi Jian.

And one of those viselike hands closed over her throat and started to squeeze.

27

IT WAS weird how those black explosions could keep happening before her eyes when her eyes were shut. Scout was fairly certain that wasn't a good sign. Her uninjured hand reached up to close over Shi Jian's wrist, but there was nothing she could do to stop the choking.

She just hoped her dogs would be okay. Bo said he liked dogs. Surely he would look out for them.

The explosions were starting to overlap, to become one tumultuous inky sea she was sinking down into.

Then the hand was gone, and Scout could finally draw a breath. Not much of one—the swollen flesh of her throat was squeezing almost as tightly as the hand had done and her windpipe felt contracted down to the size of a drinking straw—but it was better than nothing.

Hands closed on her shoulders again, and she batted at them, hurting her injured wrist but desperate not to be touched again.

"Scout!" Bo shouted, and Scout finally opened her eyes. He was looking at her with deep concern, then with relief as he saw her looking back at him. "What is going on here?"

"Your assassins tried to kill me," Scout said. Her voice was a hoarse wheeze, and every word hurt.

"No," Bo said, looking at the kids gathered around him. Some of them were still clutching at their ears, and it looked like they had tucked their weapons away along with their murderous intents, but Scout didn't trust that would last for long. "Scout, these kids are training to be spies. They learn how to fight in case their lives are in danger, but they aren't assassins."

Scout couldn't summon more words through her ravaged throat. She just looked at Bo steadily until he dropped his own eyes.

"Shi Jian?" Scout asked.

"In the brig," Bo said. "I don't understand what happened here. She must have had a reason to be choking you like that. But that doesn't sound like you either. Why would she see you as a threat?"

"I unjammed the marshal channels," Scout said.

Bo looked confused. Then he looked up at the workstation she was leaning against. He tapped at the screen and seemed to realize she was telling the truth.

"You summoned the tribunal enforcers," he said. "Why didn't you come to me first?"

"Tried that," Scout croaked. "My AI was told you were in the library. You weren't."

"I don't understand this at all," Bo said. He stood up and pressed a button on the band around his wrist. "You kids stay where you are. You're going to be confined to quarters until I get to the bottom of this."

"Yes, sir," a few of the oldest said. Not sounding at all like they had just tried to kill Scout. They also didn't sound surprised to be potentially punished, or worried about their missing leader.

They were just biding their time and waiting for the next order. And they didn't take orders from Bo. Scout had to get off this ship.

"Dogs?" Scout said suddenly, trying to get up from the ground. Bo put a restraining hand on her shoulder.

"They're here," he promised her. "Here's Shadow. Someone bring down the other one. Easy, I don't think she likes you."

Scout closed her eyes, the long night of not sleeping catching up with her. Shadow curled up beside her and Gert clamored over both of them the minute she was set down on the pit floor.

Scout dozed as the security team arrived to move the kids to their quarters. She was vaguely aware of the sounds of them being led away, but couldn't muster much interest. Her throat was throbbing, and she had to time her breathing around the throbs. It took all her concentration.

"Shi Jian has gone missing, sir," one of the officers said, and Scout forced her eyes open.

"Missing? She was just here. I pushed her off Scout myself," Bo said.

"We'll sweep the ship," the officer said and turned to give orders to his subordinates.

Scout doubted very much that they would find Shi Jian if she didn't want to be found.

"Come, Scout," Bo said, helping her to her feet. "I'll go with you to sickbay. The tribunal enforcers are on their way. They will be docking shortly, but let's get you fixed up first."

"Okay," Scout croaked, but she let her eyes slide back shut. She felt herself being lifted, placed on a floating cot with the dogs beside her.

She didn't really snap awake until she heard a soft beep and realized she was lying in a medical pod, a blast of warm air blowing across her face just slowing to a halt. Then the lid opened, and she sat up.

"How are you feeling?" Bo asked. An anxious-looking doctor in red scrubs stood behind him.

"Better," Scout said, her voice as clear as ever. "Did you find Shi Jian?"

"Not yet," Bo said, his face grim. "The tribunal enforcers have docked. They are setting up a virtual meeting with the Months. It will link up through my own audience chamber. Not a room I ever use," he said with that little nose wrinkle.

"We haven't crossed the barricade yet," Scout guessed, letting Bo help her out of the pod. The dogs had been sitting anxiously near the wall, and both charged forward at once to jump all over her.

"No, and I don't understand why," Bo said. "The lawyers can't see any hang-up, and yet the tribunal enforcers still seem to be waiting for something to happen." He shrugged. "They communicate amongst themselves handily enough, but when they try to talk to the rest of the human race, that's where it all breaks down."

Scout looked around, then found her glasses on the counter by the sink in the little examining room they were in. She slipped them on and said, "Hello, Teacher."

"Hello, Scout," Warrior said, appearing in one of the chairs. "Do you need me?"

"I just like having you around," Scout said. She saw Bo pulling a pair of glasses of his own out of his sleeve. They were round with wire frames, but his lenses were clear. He wrapped the frames around his ears and then looked up at Warrior.

"Interesting," he said. "Perhaps not surprising, given your history."

"What do you mean?" Scout asked. Bo gave a little shake of his head, glancing at the doctor standing in the room with them.

"We should get to the audience chamber," Bo said, putting a hand on her back to guide her out of the room. Despite Rona's insistence, no one tried to put leashes on the dogs. They were scarcely necessary, as anxious as the dogs were to stay near Scout.

"You don't know who to trust now," Scout guessed.

"No, I don't," Bo admitted. "I always trusted Shi Jian—since I was half your age, I've trusted her. But I don't understand what just happened. And rather than explain, she chose to disappear. I don't know what to think."

"She's the assassin I told you about," Scout said. "And all those kids—"

"She was training them to be spies," Bo said. "I didn't even like that idea, but she insisted they would get more and better intel than a grown-up ever could. And I believed her. She has done a lot of studying on such matters. I've always relied on her."

"Has she always worked for your family?" Scout asked.

"No," he said, leading her out of the brightly lit medical area into the more familiar warm wood-paneled halls of his ship. "She was a galactic marshal when I met her. She saved me from a kidnapping attempt when I was eight. My father hired her to be my personal body-guard after that. But she's more than that. She took the place of my own AI tutor when I outgrew it. She's shaped all my ways of seeing the world and what I can do in it. More, she's my right hand. Every-thing I've accomplished, it's because she knew how to take my ideas and shape them into reality. If I can't trust her… I have to get you off this ship."

Scout buried her hands deep in her pockets. Half of her stones were gone now, and she found herself a little bit sad about that. Those were Amatheon stones, little pieces of her home that she could carry with her even as she moved further and further across the galaxy. And now half of them were gone.

"Those kids are being trained to kill," Scout said. "And many people were killed by your people on *Amatheon Orbiter 1*. If not by your order, then by Shi Jian's."

"There will be a thorough investigation," Bo promised her.

"I don't know how you're going to do that," Scout said. "For all you know, *all* of your people are really hers."

Bo gave her a hard look. "You might be right about that. I'll have my father's people do it when we get to Galactic Central."

"Maybe you should leave with me," Scout said. "The tribunal enforcers may be the only people you can trust."

"Tempting," Bo said. "But no. I made this mess. I have to sort it out."

The hallway they were walking down ended in a pair of double doors, much less imposing than what the Months had leading into their audience chamber. They opened at Bo's touch, and Scout saw the ménage of tribunal enforcers assigned to Bo and Bo's lawyers already gathered there.

"This is unprecedented," the chief lawyer said the minute Bo stepped into the room. "They won't even share the content of the message with us. How can we prepare a response?"

"There isn't going to be a response," Bo said. "We're giving Scout everything she wants."

The lawyer gaped, but before he could summon any words, there was a flicker of light from all around the room. First, the other ménage of tribunal enforcers appeared, hands folded and heads down. Then the Months and their lawyers appeared at the far end of the room.

Then, almost as if an afterthought, Geeta and Emilie appeared in the middle of the room. Scout ran to their holograms, the dogs close at her heels.

"What's happening?" Emilie asked. She nearly had to shout to be heard over the lawyers converging on either side of them.

"Shut it!" Scout shouted. To her amazement, the lawyers fell silent, all turning to look at her. "There's nothing to debate. I've appealed to the tribunal enforcers for amnesty and passage out of this restricted area. None of you can say a thing about that."

"This planet and everything within its orbit is property of the Tajaki trade dynasty," the Months' lawyer said. "You have no voice in these discussions and no right to call for amnesty."

"I do, actually," Scout said. Emilie and Geeta looked as confused as any of the lawyers, but Scout's eyes were on the young tribunal enforcer, who was once more looking at her with total concentration.

"Warrior," Scout said. "What is that one saying? Can you tell me?"

Emilie's eyes tracked past Scout to Warrior standing beside her, but Geeta saw nothing.

Warrior watched the tribunal enforcer's face for a long moment. "It's a repeating message," she said at last. "It's a tricky language, but I believe they are saying this is a matter of justice."

"A matter of justice?" Emilie repeated.

Geeta looked startled. "Is that the sign?" she asked.

Scout had just been wondering the same thing. Had this tribunal enforcer been waiting for one of them to speak the countersign this whole time?

"We can get off these ships," Scout whispered to the other two. "We can leave with the tribunal enforcers. It's safer."

"I won't leave my sister," Geeta said. "The ménage assigned to the Months will keep Seeta and I safe enough."

Emilie looked deeply torn, but in the end, she took a step closer to Geeta. "I'll stick with Geeta. But Scout, you go with these tribunal enforcers. Get to the Torreses. We'll all find each other again at Galactic Central."

"Yes," Scout agreed. "Oh, also, Bo seems like he's okay, but the woman in black was working for him this whole time, only he didn't know who she really was or what she was up to right under his nose. She's disappeared again. Watch out for her; I think she wants to kill us."

"That seems to be her thing," Geeta said. "Stay safe."

"You too," Scout said, wishing she could give her friends one last hug, but at the moment they were just light and sound, their bodies too far away to be touched.

"If you girls are quite done?" Bo's lawyer prompted, and Scout realized everyone was glaring at them as they whispered together. She straightened her back, throwing her braid back over her shoulder.

"Oh, and it's a good look," Emilie said, her eyes making an exaggerated sweep of Scout from head to toe. Just like Emilie, to want to get one last whisper in.

"It suits you," Geeta agreed. "We'll see you soon."

"I hope so," Scout said. She looked around, made sure her dogs were still close beside her, and looked to the ménages of tribunal enforcers who had all stepped closer around her.

"I ask for amnesty and passage out of this restricted system," Scout said, looking to the youngest tribunal enforcer. "It's a matter of justice. But more, it's a matter of sovereignty. The people of Amatheon do not recognize the Tajaki trade dynasty as their owners, employers, or masters, or as having any power over them."

The young tribunal enforcer smiled. That expression was clear enough, and Scout returned it.

Jun Tajaki shrieked in rage, a sound abruptly cut off as the transmission ended and Scout was once more in a half-empty audience chamber with Bo and his people.

"I hope we'll stay in contact," Bo said as he walked with Scout and the tribunal enforcers back to the airlock. "I'm so very sorry. I did think you'd be safe here."

"I believe you," Scout said. "Contact me every day so I know you're all right."

"It's going to be lonely for you, traveling with this crew," Bo said. "They never speak out loud. Sometimes they get surprised into laughing. It's… not pleasant."

"I don't have far to go," Scout said. "People are waiting for me on the other side."

She hoped that was true, that the Torreses had made it all the way to the barricade before being unable to continue. That they still waited for her. She wasn't looking forward to flying in a transparent ship with a crew of people she couldn't talk with. Hopefully, it would be a short trip, followed by another trip across an airlock.

"Come, dogs," Scout said, summoning her dogs close to her side. Then they stepped out together, into the long white hallway that appeared to open up onto space itself. It was disorienting to look at, and she wasn't even in it yet. But she didn't slow her steps, and she didn't look back.

Time to face the next adventure.

CHECK OUT BOOK FIVE!

The Travels of Scout Shannon continues in book five, Over Freezing Altitudes.

Having escaped yet another closing trap, Scout Shannon finds herself on a snowbound mountaintop far from civilization. With assassins eager to kill her, laying low on an alien world is the smartest play.

But wherever Scout goes, trouble follows. And a hamlet in the mountains gets far more remote when girl assassins destroy the only means back to civilization.

Now Scout and her dogs face a long, cold climb back to the frozen star port city, her only guide, a girl whose sister Scout killed when fighting for her life. Can she get to safety before the girl learns the truth about Scout? And what secrets of her own is this strange girl keeping?

"Over Freezing Altitudes" the fifth book in "The Travels of Scout Shannon" series, a young adult science fiction novel for fans of resourceful heroines, survival in extreme environments, girl assassins and loyal dog sidekicks.

Over Freezing Altitudes, the fifth book in the Travels of Scout Shannon. Check it out!

NEW SERIES: THE FORGOTTEN PLANET

Coming soon from Ratatoskr Press Books, the new YA sci-fi series THE FORGOTTEN PLANET starts with book 1: Raiding the Forgotten Derelict.

History sleeps beneath them all, but only she sees it.

Lafayette Eloi always knew her parents thought differently from others. They kept their books buried beneath her mother's house. They spoke an old language in the dead of night, whispering behind closed doors and bolted shutters. She grew up in a village where no one was related to her, and she never knew why.

Then, after her mother died, her father came to fetch her. Now she and her mother's dog assist her father in his work. The work discussed in whispers in the dark. The work that had cost Lafayette so much all her young life.

But now she learns just how much her father's work means to their entire world. Only no one knows anything about it. Only her father. And only Lafayette.

Because the work that consumed her father's entire life and her mother's too now nibbles at the fringe's of Lafayette's own life. And she cannot refuse its call.

Raiding the Forgotten Derelict, first book in the new YA sci-fu series THE FORGOTTEN PLANET, available in September 2024 from Ratatoskr Press Books.

COMPLETE SERIES: THE RITCHIE AND FITZ SCI-FI MURDER MYSTERIES

The Ritchie and Fitz Sci-Fi Murder Mysteries starts with Murder on the Intergalactic Railway.

For Murdina Ritchie, acceptance at the Oymyakon Foreign Service Academy means one last chance at her dream of becoming a diplomat for the Union of Free Worlds. For Shackleton Fitz IV, it represents his last chance not to fail out of military service entirely.

Strange that fate should throw them together now, among the last group of students admitted after the start of the semester. They had once shared the strongest of friendships. But that all ended a long time ago.

But when an insufferable but politically important woman turns up murdered, the two agree to put their differences aside and work together to solve the case.

Because the murderer might strike again. But more importantly, solving a murder would just have to impress the dour colonel who clearly thinks neither of them belong at his academy.

Murder on the Intergalactic Railway, the first book in the Ritchie and Fitz Sci-Fi Murder Mysteries.

COMPLETE SERIES: THE TRAVELS OF SCOUT SHANNON

The complete six-book series THE TRAVELS OF SCOUT SHANNON begin with book one, Under Falling Skies.

Scout Shannon's whole family died the day the Space Farers dropped an asteroid on their domed city. Now she lives alone, out in the wild with only her dogs for company. She prefers it that way.

But Scout finds herself at a crossroads. One road leads back to a quiet life snug under the protective dome of a city. The other road leads to a life in the rebellion, a life of adventure and excitement but also danger. Dare she try to find the rebels hiding in the hills?

Then a chance encounter with a stranger from the other side of the galaxy threatens to derail what remains of Scout's life. The entire galaxy awaits her, if she survives the next four days.

"Under Falling Skies", a young adult science fiction novel, set on a remote planet with a distinctly Old West feel. For fans of gunslinging women and young girl assassins. And dogs.

Under Falling Skies, the first book in THE TRAVELS OF SCOUT SHANNON, available everywhere now.

SCI-FI SERIAL PODCAST!

Check out my new monthly podcast of serialized science fiction: THE TALES OF THE CHAI MAKHANI TRIO!

Elyot loathes the massive Commonwealth ships that hover menacingly over his home world of Adghal. He hates the Commonwealth enforcers who harass the populace even more. But with his mother missing and presumed dead, Elyot keeps his head down and strives to avoid notice. And he succeeds until the day two strangers enter his life...

New episodes of this sci-fi serial drop every 1st of the month.

Now streaming on Apple Podcasts, Google Podcasts, Spotify, Stitcher and more. Also available in eBook and print everywhere books or sold. For a complete episode listing, check out the page on my website.

ALSO FROM KATE MACLEOD

Love heists and capers? Then check out my new series, THE VIC HARPER CAPERS. The action starts with the novella THE THIRD POLE JOB.

Vic Harper and her gang retired wealthy from their life of thievery and heists. Whether in a luxury condo overlooking the river in Minneapolis or in a modernist mansion built into the side of a mountain in Colorado, life comes easy now.

Perhaps too easy.

When an old friend asks for a favor his niece, Vic and her mentor Chase Woodward leap at the chance to relieve a little of the boredom. But a quick bit of B&E in a wealthy suburb of Chicago leads to an even greater challenge.

The prize? Nothing much. Just the opportunity to level a playing field for their friend's niece.

But the heist? May prove to be their toughest ever. Because to get to the prize, they'll have to climb a mountain.

And not just any mountain. Their prize waits on the summit of Mount Everest.

THE THIRD POLE JOB, the first novella in the Vic Harper Caper series. For those who love capers, heists and other impossible missions.

ALSO FROM RATATOSKR PRESS

Also from Ratatoskr Press, The Witches Three Cozy Mystery Series by Cate Martin, a mix of mystery and magic that begins with Book 1: Charm School.

Amanda Clarke thinks of herself as perfectly ordinary in every way. Just a small-town girl who serves breakfast all day in a little diner nestled next to the highway, nothing but dairy farms for miles around. She fits in there.

But then an old woman she never met dies, and Amanda was named in her will. Now Amanda packs a bag and heads to the big city, to Miss Zenobia Weekes' Charm School for Exceptional Young Ladies. And it's not in just any neighborhood. No, she finds herself on Summit Avenue in St. Paul, a street lined with gorgeous old houses, the former homes of lumber barons, railroad millionaires, even the writer F. Scott Fitzgerald. Why, Amanda can practically hear the jazz music still playing across the decades.

Scratch that. The music really, literally, still plays in the backyard of the charm school. Because the house stretches across time itself. Without a witch to protect this tear in the fabric of the world, anything can spill over. Like music.

Or like murder.

The complete series is out now, and it all starts with Charm School.

FREE EBOOK!

Like exclusive, free content?

To get two prequel short stories to THE RITCHIE AND FITZ SCI-FI MURDER MYSTERIES as well as a bonus prequel novelette to the completed six-book series THE TRAVELS OF SCOUT SHANNON, signup for my monthly newsletter at KateMacLeodWrites.com.

Thank you!

ABOUT THE AUTHOR

Photograph © 2016 Jonathan Conklin

Kate MacLeod has written stories which have appeared in Analog, Strange Horizons and Mythic Delirium, among other places. She is also the author of two young adult science fictions series: The Travels of Scout Shannon, and The Ritchie and Fitz Sci-Fi Murder Mysteries. She also contributes to a serialized science fiction podcast called The Tales of the Chai Makhani Trio. She currently lives in Minneapolis, Minnesota.

Find out more about the author and sign up for her newsletter at KateMacLeodWrites.com.

ALSO BY KATE MACLEOD

Novels

The Slums of the Solar System:

Mitwa

The Mars of Malcontents

The Whole World for Each

Books 1-3 Box Set

The Travels of Scout Shannon:

Under Falling Skies

In Quaking Hills

Among Treacherous Stars

Against Impassable Barriers

Over Freezing Altitudes

At Galactic Central

The Travels of Scout Shannon Books 1-3

The Travels of Scout Shannon Books 4-6

The Travels of Scout Shannon Books 1-6

The Ritchie and Fitz Sci-Fi Murder Mysteries:

Murder on the Intergalactic Railway

Murder in the Skies

Body in the Catacombs

Death on the Summit

An Undiplomatic Murder

A Lethal Betrayal

The Forgotten Planet

Raiding the Forgotten Derelict (Forthcoming September 2024)

Sci-Fi Novellas